Khan

Bowen Boys Book 2

By

Kathi S. Barton

World Castle Publishing

Kathi S. Barton

WCP

World Castle Publishing
Pensacola, Florida

Copyright © Kathi S. Barton 2013
ISBN: 9781939865502
First Edition World Castle Publishing June 1, 2013
http://www.worldcastlepublishing.com

Cover: Karen Fuller
Editor: Brieanna Robertson

Kathi S. Barton

Chapter One

Khan looked out the back door to his home and watched the deer playing. He'd not been out much and they'd made a playground of his yard. He turned away from them when he felt his cat snarl at him. He wanted to go out and hunt them down. Khan walked into his living room and looked around.

His house was a sty. It probably smelled bad too, but he was so far gone in that department that, on his own, he didn't notice it. That was one of the reasons he'd told his mom to stay away. She'd hang him out to dry if she could see this place. But he was in hiding.

His brother and his mate had left for their honeymoon three weeks ago. And in all that time, he'd not left his house. Not even to go out and run with his brothers. His mail he'd get well after dark and then only if he ran out, got it, and returned quickly. He hated doing this, but he was not meeting his mate.

Caitlynne, his brother Walker's mate, had told him he was going to meet her and she would be human. She wasn't clairvoyant or anything, but she'd been predicting that it would happen every day he talked to them. He liked the girl well enough, but was still not going to bring another human in this group. So he'd been hiding.

The phone ringing startled him and he ignored it. It was one of his brothers again, and he wasn't in the mood to talk yet. He was staying right here until everyone got the idea that he wasn't going to mate with anyone and that they should leave him the hell alone. He nearly screamed when someone lay on the doorbell, ringing the sucker like it was their job.

Opening the door, he was ready to snarl at the person there when he was suddenly engulfed in a pair of female arms and she was kissing him on the cheeks. Khan tried in vain to pull her off him, but Caitlynne was a lot stronger than she looked. Finally, when he saw Walker, he told his brother to control his female.

"Female, huh? I guess we haven't moved on to the first name thing yet. No matter. I still missed you." She walked in the house and went to his living room as if she owned it. Maybe she kinda did. He wanted to talk to her about that too.

"Come on in. Make yourself at home, why don't you?" He glared at Walker when he laughed. "This isn't funny. I told you when you called me this morning to stay the fuck away. What are you doing here anyway?"

"You stink."

Khan growled at her.

"And your house looks like a frat house. Though I'm thinking that a frat house might smell better. What the fuck have you been doing?"

"I've been minding my own business like I wish the hell you did. Get out of there." He jerked the box of cereal from her and put it with the others. "Tell me what you want, then leave. I think I've made it perfectly clear that my home is—"

"Yeah, yeah, it's yours. So what? We have to talk to you and I can't do it in here. Not unless you want me to decorate with puke. Christ, I thought you had more balls than to hide away like some sort of hermit." She moved to the kitchen and out of the living room. "I'm waiting on you."

Khan looked at Walker, who hadn't said a word and was smiling like a sap. He didn't know whether to punch him in the nose for siccing Caitlynne on him or kick him out with her.

"You'd better go in there. If it looks half as bad as this room, she's probably calling a cleaning crew."

Khan looked at the mess and knew that it was worse in the kitchen. He took off after her.

"Yes. Today, if possible. I'll pay extra. And you might want to bring in extra help. It's been awhile." He could only stare at her when she hung up the phone. "You should be ashamed of yourself for this. What the fuck would your mom say?"

"You do know that I'm not going to let them in, don't you? You might as well call them back and tell them not to come. My house is mine." She smiled and sat down. "Caitlynne, I'm not kidding you."

"You know, that's the really sad part. I know you're not. But I can't visit you in this place. I will really be sick everywhere." Walker came into the room and smiled at her. "We have something to tell you. You might want to sit down."

He sat. He knew that there were battles to win with her, not that he remembered winning any, but he sat. When she told him her news, he was going to demand that she call the cleaning crew back, and then he was going to discuss the money in his account.

"We're going to have a baby."

Khan opened his mouth and closed it twice before he looked at Walker.

"See, I told you he'd be speechless."

She stood up again and started stacking dishes. He could smell that she was nervous and didn't say anything as she continued to clean. Walker sat beside him and stacked the dishes in front of both of them as he started talking.

"We knew before we left, but didn't want to tell anyone. She was nervous that no one would let her go on our honeymoon."

Khan nodded, took the stack of dishes that Walker handed him, and gave them to Caitlynne.

"We wanted to tell you first, then we'd all go over to Mom and Dad's and tell everyone there. We stopped here because we've heard that you've become something of a recluse."

"I've been trying to get things together." Khan flushed when his brother raised a brow at him and looked around. "Cleaning up was low on my list."

Caitlynne snorted, and Walker laughed. "It looks to me like your list didn't include cleaning at all. Why didn't you hire someone to come in and clean? You know that there was enough money to do that, you moron."

That made him remember his bank statement. "You put money in my account and I want you to take it out. And my bills too. I want you to tell whoever is getting them and paying them to stop that too. I pay my own way."

"Of course you do." He decided that it was the pat on his head like he was ten years old that made him grind his teeth at her. "Unless you want me to kick your ass, I would take it down a notch. I'm a little hormonal right now and you've not said one word about the baby. Are you so pigheaded that you can't even be happy for us?"

Then Caitlynne Bowen did something he would never have thought of seeing her do. She burst into tears. Walker didn't even bat an eye, but picked her up, dirty dishrag and all, and held her. Khan was glad he'd been sitting down or he might have fallen.

"She's been having a hard time with her emotions. I told her it would pass, but it's difficult for her."

Khan nodded at his brother's explanation.

"She isn't as bad as she was a week ago, but we're still having issues."

"I am not. I'm perfectly fine until some asshole makes me upset." She stood up and began where she'd left off cleaning. "As for your money. You can do whatever you want with it. It's yours, but know this; I will not stop doing what I'm doing. I'm enjoying myself. And you would too if you got out of this house."

She went to answer the door and he didn't move. Khan knew it was the cleaning service and wondered how much money she promised them to get here in an hour. He stood up when he heard them coming toward where they were. "I want to go on a run. Now, I want to go now." He moved to the door and out it before he realized that Walker was coming with him. Good, he'd have someone to help him look for women...strangers.

They had been in the woods for nearly an hour when he finally lay down. Walker and he had run for most of that time without saying much more than, "go this way," or, "okay." He hadn't realized how much he needed this until the panic of someone being in his house made him run.

"She feels bad because she ran you from your house. I told her it was because you felt embarrassed at the mess more than anything." They had shifted and were near the lake that ran along all their houses. "She said to tell you that if you wait another couple of hours, the house will be spotless and she'll be gone."

Khan didn't look at Walker, but he did feel the need to explain. He picked up a handful of small stones and began skipping them across the still water. He had to talk to someone. "I've been out of my mind with worry that my mate will show up at the door and she'll be human." He skipped two more stones waiting for his brother to say something.

"I don't know what to tell you, Khan, but you staying in the house all the time and living like that won't keep you from meeting her. I think there are bigger forces at work here than you hiding in your house." He watched as Walker's rock skipped seventeen times. "Mom called me before we left France."

He figured she would call him sooner or later. "What did she tell you? That I need to be committed? That I've gone over the deep end? I assure you that I haven't."

Walker didn't comment, for which Khan was grateful. They started back toward the house an hour later. Khan knew that he'd hurt Caitlynne and was sorry for that, but she'd frightened him with her predictions.

"If I meet my mate and she's just what Caitlynne said she'd be, I'm never going to live it down, am I?" Khan looked at Walker when he laughed.

"Nope. And like she told you months ago, she'll gloat until you tell her that she was right." They were near the house now and he could see the five vans and two cars in the driveway. It looked like she'd called in the entire company.

"I should probably just tell her she was right all along if that happens." Walker agreed, and they both watched as people, mostly women dressed in jeans and t-shirts, poured from his house. "Walker?"

"I know, Khan. I know you're afraid of getting hurt again, and I don't blame you, but if you just give the girl, any girl, a chance, you'll see it's pretty fucking wonderful."

~~~

George couldn't stop smiling. A grandchild. Walker and Caitlynne were going to give him a grandchild. He grinned at his mate and held her hand. They were going to spoil it rotten.

He looked over at Khan and realized how much weight his son had lost. He would say right around thirty pounds if he had to guess. Weight that he didn't need to lose. Caitlynne sat down next to him and handed him a brightly wrapped gift. She'd been handing them out since they got up from the table. This was his third or fourth one.

"You have to stop this. You've given us so much." He tore into the paper like a little kid. He loved getting presents.

"I know, you hate all this hoopla. But we had fun shopping, and even though I've been there a lot with business and all, this was the first time I was actually there to have fun." She handed a similarly wrapped package to Corrine. "Did you know that they love cats in Japan? That's where we got this one."

It was a medallion. He held it up to the light and saw the cat etched on it. He could see the dark colors and knew it was a panther. Corrine had one as well. Hers was on a chain to wear around her neck, and his was attached to a beautiful pocket watch. George kissed her on the cheek as he put it in his pocket.

He watched her move around the room. Her belly was just beginning to poof out. He hadn't said anything about it because she seemed a bit touchy about everything. When he'd told her that he'd missed her, for instance, she'd cried. And when Corrine had handed her a fruit salad instead of leaf lettuce like they had, she'd cried again. Walker told them she was all right, just hormonal. He hoped that was all it was.

Walker was watching her too. He looked so happy that it was all George could do not to stand up and do a jig. And the fact that they'd brought Khan over with them had him as happy as a lark. He looked over at Corrine when she tugged on his arm.

"You old fool, you should listen to them. I don't know what has gotten into them." She nodded toward Reed and Marc. "They fight much more and I'm going to send them to the shed."

The boys had been arguing about one thing or another for the better part of a week. He hadn't been able to get either one of them to tell him what it was about, but he'd had enough. They were upsetting their mother. Before he could stand and take charge, Caitlynne did.

She knocked the chair legs out from under Marc and then stepped on his head. Before Reed could get out of her reach, she had him down as well. He knew that neither of them would hurt her, but he was just standing up to tell her to let him take care of it when Khan simply stood up.

"I've only been here for a little over two hours and you have been biting at each other ever since. What the fuck is going on?" She pulled a gun out and pointed it at Reed when he started to stand up. "I'm not in the mood to fuck with you, young man. Either you two tell me or I'll start shooting manly parts. I don't believe those heal all that well from what I've heard."

"He said that you're going to keep me from working with the CIA and that you had no intentions of letting me before you left here." Reed sounded more hurt than mad, and she apparently knew it too.

"So instead of coming to me and asking, you let him bait you into being pissy at our homecoming? You're an idiot." She lifted her foot off of Marc's face long enough to look at him then put it back. "And you. What the fuck? You have nothing better to do than fuck with him? You want me to find you something to do?"

"No. But…" Marc looked at his brother then up at her, and George had an idea what was going to spill from his son's mouth. "Why does he get a job like that when I don't?"

She lifted her foot off him and put her gun away. When she told them both to stand up, she stepped back from them and crossed her arms over her chest. She was tapping her foot hard, and he knew she was pissed.

"You want a job. Well, good for you. I thought you had one. Or is that little investigative thing you got going on not a job? You sit around your office all day and eat bon-bons?" He shook his head and glared at her. "Again, why didn't you come to me and ask?"

"You've been away." Marc looked up at his brother and then back at the floor. "I'm sorry, but I don't really have anything to do. My business pretty much runs itself now, and with the money you put into my account, I don't have to stress about every little thing. I'm bored."

He had to hand it to her, she was good. When she started pacing the room, George noticed that his other sons, Dylan and Sebastian, both sat near Marc and Reed. It seemed that each of them wanted a job.

"And what the hell am I supposed to do with four little boys?" Each of them looked ready to protest, but she stopped them with a raised hand. "You're boys. Only a boy would sit around and whine about how he's got nothing to do. Only little kids would pick at each other until they got their asses kicked only to start all over pissing another kid off. You want a job? Then fucking earn it. You think I got mine handed to me? No, I did not. I had to go to college and work my ass off. You think it was easy for a woman to get to where I am right now? No, it fucking wasn't."

Each of them dropped their heads and wouldn't look at her. George glanced over at his other two sons and was happy to see them laughing. Quietly, but they were laughing. His mate touched his shoulder.

"She'll make a great mother. She might want to clean up her language a bit, but she'll love them."

George nodded at Corrine's observation.

"I can't wait to hold him."

George didn't want to say anything, but he wanted a granddaughter. He had enough boys. He loved them, but wanted a little granddaughter to spoil and have hang out with him. He looked over at Corrine and started to tell her his dreams when Caitlynne spoke again.

"Starting tomorrow morning, each of you will report to the construction crew on Walker's land. And if I hear of one tiny little argument, I will make your lives a living hell for a month." Marc started to protest, but stopped. George couldn't see Caitlynne's face, but he was sure she was giving him that brow thing.

He'd seen her do it to Walker. She would simply raise her pretty eyebrow at him and he'd be bending over backwards to make her happy. His boys did it as well, but she had a certain power over them they didn't quite understand yet. It was the Mom factor.

Every woman had it, and when breeding like she was, it was something to behold. George watched the boys sit there for a few minutes longer after Caitlynne moved out of the room. He nearly went after her when Khan walked up to the boys.

"You made her cry, are you happy?" Each of them looked to where she'd gone before dropping their heads again. "If I hear that you did this again, I will hunt each of you down and make you regret it for the rest of your days. Do I make myself understood?"

They said that they did and nodded. Walker didn't even have to speak to them, but looked down on them. Shame was the worst kind of punishment, and these two had done a number on their brothers. George sat back on the couch and decided that he was going to go out to the site himself to see what the boys would do to please their sister-in-law.

Chapter Two

Marc watched his brother come toward him. It wasn't until he moved to the left to answer a nurse that he noticed that he brought Caitlynne with him. This was not going to go as well as he'd hoped. She, of course, came straight at him. And she did not look like she was happy.

"Where is she?"

He didn't answer, but nodded to Walker.

"He told me that you were beat to shit and that your partner was as well. Is this your way of getting out of work tomorrow?"

He'd forgotten about that. "No. And that would be today. I was the only person left to go on this and she needed backup. More than us apparently."

The city had asked him to investigate the local trash company. People were complaining about things not being picked up and trashcans being tossed around the street so that they'd been hit by other cars. What he'd found tonight was that the company was also entering garages and taking things.

"They let me take her as a patient. But as I told you on the phone, we're leaving day after tomorrow, so you either have to find another doctor for her or we'll have to think of something else." Walker was pulling on a lab coat and had a stethoscope in his hand as he spoke. "You might want to consider Doctor Tanner. He's—"

"She's going to come home with me." They both looked at him wide-eyed. "If he finds her again—and if she stays here, he will—he said he'd kill her. I like this girl, and I won't let some asswipe hurt her again."

Monica Preston worked for his firm. She'd not been there long, but she had proven to be a good worker and a great investigator. Marc had hired her as someone to answer phones and work the office. He discovered her worth when it only took her fifteen minutes to solve a problem for a client that they'd been working on for weeks. He'd promoted her and hadn't regretted it since.

"Marc, is she your…"

Marc looked at his brother and wondered what he was talking about. Then it hit him. "No. Christ no. I like her and all, but no, she's not my mate." He glanced toward the room where she was. "But I do feel protective of her. Very much so. I don't know what it is, but I can't let anything happen to her.

Walker went to see to her, and Marc and Caitlynne followed him. His breath caught every time he saw her. Christ, her boyfriend had done a number on her. He was glad he'd been there because he was able to scare him off, but by the time he'd figured out what was going on, it had been too late.

Her face was all that he could see of her right now, but back at the scene, he'd looked her over. Two broken ribs, he thought, and her fingers had been stomped on. Her left eye was swollen shut and the other filled with blood. He thought her lower lip was going to need stitches, but didn't know for sure because there was so much blood all over her. He cringed when Caitlynne started barking questions at her.

"Did you know that this man was capable of doing this to you?"

Monica nodded.

"Then tell me why you'd stay with the mother fucker. Is this how you get your jollies?"

Monica wasn't normally an aggressive person, but she came up off the bed at Caitlynne in a heartbeat. "You have no idea what you're talking about. I've had five restraining orders against him in the past four months. I moved here to get away from him. Again. He did this because he thinks in his twisted fucking mind that I belong to him and goes into a rage whenever I try to make it so he stays away. You think of some way to make this stop and I'm all for it."

She staggered, and Caitlynne grabbed for her. When Monica cried out in pain, both he and Walker stepped forward. But the look on her face had them both step back. She was afraid of them.

"Come on. Let's get you taken care of." Caitlynne helped her back into the bed. "I'm sorry for pissing you off, but you seemed to need it. Now we can get the prick and take care of him. Can you shoot a gun?"

Walker laughed, and so did Marc. The question had been so calmly asked that it startled Monica. The look on her face was priceless. She told Caitlynne no, but she'd thought of it. Caitlynne assured her that she'd teach her how the next time she was in town.

When Monica was safely in the bed, Caitlynne left the room. When Marc started after her, Walker shook his head and turned to Monica. It wasn't until he whispered to him mind that she was okay, just emotional that he understood how hard this might be on her.

"Is she all right? I didn't mean to upset her."

Walker smiled at Monica as Marc moved to the little chair next to the bed. "She's fine. Pregnant, that's all. She gets very emotional and she's not used to it." Walker asked her to lay back. "Let me make sure nothing is broken and get you stitched up. Has anyone talked to you about where you're going to stay?"

Monica glanced at him and he nodded. "Marc said I could stay at his house. I know he's your brother and all, but I won't take advantage of his good nature. I just need a place to stay until I can move on. I can't bring Tony's crap into your family."

The examination took thirty minutes. When Walker asked him to step out so he could check the rest of her out, Marc went to find Caitlynne. She was in the lounge making calls. Her ever-present laptop sat on the little table in front of her. She smiled as she closed the phone when he walked up.

"I'm doing phone interviews for a secretary. I hate this shit. I want to be out on the job, not stuck inside doing crap work. Do you know how many phone calls I got on my honeymoon? Over five hundred. I'm already hating this."

He knew she wasn't and that she'd be very good at being the director of the CIA. He also knew that she'd already been able to solve a major crime wave hitting the DC area while she'd been away. Marc was very proud of his sister-in-law.

"When did she start working for you?" He told her what he knew about her, knowing that if he didn't, she'd go and ask Monica.

"She's been living here since June, right about the time you and Walker met. She applied to work for me around that time too. I'd been looking for someone to answer phones and she fit it. But I figured out she was a little more than that and hired her as one of my investigators. She's that good."

Caitlynne nodded. "And the man? Her stalker? What do you know about him? Has he hurt her before since she's been working for you?"

Marc started to say no, but thinking on it, he thought maybe he had. "I believe so, but she's never said anything. Last week, she gave me her notice. Said she had to go and take care of a very sick mother. I never thought anything about it until just now. She was running again."

"I would think so. Her parents are deceased. She has one brother, but he's not worth much. No other relatives that I can find. She's moved a lot over the past fifteen months. And at each place she lands, she racks up a hospital bill that she can't afford but makes payments on. She's made monthly payments to each place since this started."

Marc wasn't surprised that she had so much information on the girl. "I can't let her go. I don't know what it is about her, but something makes me want to protect her at all costs." He glanced at her when she snorted. "It's kind of the same feeling I have when it comes to you. Most of the time, I want to strangle you, but there are times when I want to make sure you're all right."

He didn't say anything when she looked away. He knew that she was dealing with her emotions. When she turned back to him, she was grinning. He was almost ready to cup himself when she reached over and patted his leg.

"I love you too, moron. But this feeling? Is it a cat thing or something else? You said she wasn't your mate. How sure are you of that?" He told her he was positive. "Then we have to figure out what it is and keep her here until we do. She's going to bolt at the first opportunity, you know that, right? I would if I was her."

Marc was as sure of that as he was she wasn't his mate and told her so. Walker came out a few minutes later. She was being released into Walker's care and they were taking her to his house. Marc was suddenly glad for the extra help that came in daily to clean up after him. His house used to be a natural growing ground for mushrooms and other fungi.

~~~

Monica looked at the couple who was helping her. Mrs. Bowen, as Caitlynne had told her to call her, was very beautiful, and her husband, the doctor, was very kind. She hadn't known what to think of the woman when she'd snapped at her, but knew what she'd been doing. She had taken her out of her funk of being a failure.

Monica felt like that a lot lately. Every time she would think that she'd shaken Tony Barr, he would show up like a bad penny. A very painful bad penny. She looked around the room she'd been given and wondered how long it would be before she could make her escape.

She'd never had a boss like Marc. He was really nice and was always telling her what a great job she was doing. All the people who worked for him said he was very fair and never made them feel like he was better than them. Him coming to work the trash sting was a surprise. She'd been slated to work with David, but he'd come down with the flu.

"Okay. I have to go and do my community service for Caitlynne. She's a real hard ass and I screwed up." Marc sat on the bed next to her and handed her a reader and the remote. "There's everything you'd want to see on the television and that thing is yours. I got two for my birthday and I haven't even opened it yet. I think that Khan said there's a fifty dollar credit on it so go for—"

"I can't take your gift." He laughed at her. "I'm serious. I can't take a gift that you got for your birthday. It's not right."

"But you see I don't need it so I'm gifting it to you. That's what Khan said to do with it. I asked him for the

22

receipt and he didn't have it. He told me to give it away." He handed it to her. "I got something else from him. I swear. Take it."

She took it to use, but wouldn't take it with her. She ran her hand over the box and looked up at him as he left the room. Monica thought there wasn't a nicer man she knew and wished that she'd met him a long time ago.

Turning on the television to keep her company, she turned it down low. The place where she had been staying had told her that she had to move out. Apparently, Tony had been by there first and had made a mess of things for her. Marc hadn't told her what he'd done, but she knew from past "visits" from him that he more than likely trashed the place. She still wondered how he'd found her on the trash truck.

The knock at the door startled her and she sat up. Looking at the bedside clock, she realized that she'd dozed off. A pretty young woman walked in with a large tray. She smiled at her as she sat it across her lap.

"Mr. Marc said you might be a little hungry and he said to bring you something light. I wasn't sure what you might like so I brought you a little of everything." She sat down in the chair. "My name is Sally. I'm his day help."

Monica told her who she was and how she knew Marc. She wasn't really sure what day help was, but assumed that it was a cleaning person. A cleaning person who could cook. Everything smelled delicious. And after her first sip of the beef barley soup, she knew she'd have to eat it all.

Sally didn't say anything while she ate. She simply watched the television and rocked. Monica didn't know why, but she felt very comfortable with her and didn't need to explain to her what she was doing there and why she was beat to hell and back. When she lifted the tray off her, Sally helped her to the bathroom.

"I've not taken Marc's bed, have I?" She had stopped in the doorway to the huge bath when that thought occurred to her. "I can go somewhere else if I have. I won't put him out of his bed."

"No, ma'am. This is one of the spares. He has three extras. This one has a full bath including a tub, and that's why you're in here. Doctor Walker said you might want a lay-down bath later."

Monica nodded and asked to be left alone to use the toilet. She had avoided looking at herself the last time he'd beaten her up, but this time she had no choice. The mirror over the sink was huge. She nearly cried when she looked at the woman staring back at her.

Her lower lip had been taped up. Walker said that stitches would leave a bigger scar so he'd put butterfly strips on it. There were three there and five over her left brow. Her right eye was filled with blood, and though it hurt a little, it looked a lot worse. She gently touched the bruising under it and winced at the pain. There was blood in her hair too, and she felt the tender knot there. She wanted a shower to wash off everything he'd done to her.

She knew that wasn't possible, but she needed to be clean. Opening the door a little, she told Sally that she felt great and was taking a shower. The girl didn't look like she thought that was a good idea and asked her to wait. But Monica closed the door and locked it. She needed this.

As soon as the hot water steamed up the mirror, she took off the shirt she'd been given. Trying not to look at herself, she stepped into the hot water. Heaven. She decided that this was the best decision she'd made in a while.

After washing her hair twice, she was beginning to feel a little lightheaded. Holding onto the tile walls, she tried to take shallow breaths until the feeling passed. When she realized she wasn't going to be able to stand much longer, she slid to the shower floor. Nope, she was done in.

When an urgent knock sounded at the door, she whimpered. She didn't have the strength to answer. Everything was fading and she knew that at any moment she was going to faint. When the door crashed open, she felt her head roll back, and she looked up at the most beautiful furious man she'd ever seen. And man, could he cuss up a storm.

He scooped her up and held her to him. She wanted to tell him she was fine, but knew it for the lie it was. When he took her into the bedroom, she saw Sally and wondered about the look on her face. The woman looked pale as a sheet. The man put her down on the bed and she was sure that he'd licked her neck.

"Don't eat me, please? I hurt too much now." Monica had a moment to wonder why he went stiff when she realized what she said. "I can manage from here, thank you."

"What the hell were you thinking? Didn't Walker tell you to take a bath? And who locks a door on someone when they're this weak?" She wanted to brain the man standing over her, but he continued. "You're naked."

"Of course I am, you moron. Who takes a shower in their clothes?" Now that she was out of the hot water, she was regaining her strength. "And in case you didn't notice, I'm a big girl and can make decisions on my own without the help of a big man. Why don't you go back to the cave you came from and leave me the hell alone? And you're paying for that door too." Monica had never spoken to anyone like that before, but found she couldn't be upset about it now. The man was a bastard and she wasn't going to take it from him. When Sally cleared her throat, they both looked at her.

"I have you another shirt, miss. It's another one of Mr. Marc's."

The man took it from her and tossed it across the room. He told Sally to get out.

Sally took off like the hounds of hell were after her. Reaching for the sheet, Monica tried to cover her body and glared up at the man when he continued to stare at her.

"I want you to get out of here. I'm in Mr. Marc's house and he'll—"

"You're human, aren't you?"

She stared at him. What the hell else would she be? She asked him this, then said, "You know, I don't really care. You should leave. While I appreciate you doing what you did, as you can see, I'm fine now. Thank you again." He didn't move.

"Who did this to you?" He tore the sheet from her and looked over her body. "Who hurt you like this? And where do I find him?"

Monica was afraid. Not for herself, but for any person who crossed this man. She flinched when he dropped to his knees, and when he reached out and cupped her head, she was sure he was…she had a feeling he was going to tear her throat out. But all he said was he wouldn't hurt her.

His breath on her throat made her dizzy. It made her want to bring him closer and have him never stop. When he ran his tongue down her throat to her collarbone, she moaned. Before she could do anything stupid like reach for him, he stood up and backed away.

"I didn't touch you. You're the one that—" She took several deep breaths even though it hurt her badly. "I don't know who you are, but I would like for you to leave me alone, please. I'm…I'm going to be gone soon and I don't want to cause Marc any problems."

He didn't move except to pick up the shirt and tear it in half. When he tossed the sheet at her, she quickly covered herself up and waited for his next move. When he spoke this time, she knew that man was off his rocker.

"Don't let anyone else touch you. If they do, then I'll hurt them. And don't think you're going to stay here either. As soon as possible, I'm having you moved." He turned to the door then looked back at her over his shoulder. "I don't want you."

Then he was gone.

Monica looked around the room and then at the sheet. Blood stained it in a couple of places, and she knew it was because she had opened her wounds. She wiped at the tears on her face she hadn't realized were falling and thought of the man. He didn't want her. She had no idea why that hurt her so much, but it did. And when Sally came back in the room and helped her into another shirt, Monica rolled to her side and shut her out. Sobbing, she fell asleep.

Kathi S. Barton

28

Chapter Three

Khan sat in the kitchen of Marc's house and waited. He knew where he was and could have gone there, but he couldn't leave just yet. Anger boiled over him like a summer storm, and he didn't trust himself with anyone yet. He glanced up to the ceiling to where he knew the girl was and glared. His fucking mate.

When Sally had called him and told him that she couldn't get the door to open and she was afraid that the woman she'd been caring for was dead, he hadn't thought, but had shifted and gone to Marc's home. He was sure it was Caitlynne and that she'd fallen, but when he'd gotten to the bedroom and saw the blood, her scent hit him. Kicking open the door happened before he could get a hold on his cat and then he was picking her up. Now he'd tasted her. Not once, but twice, and he wanted more.

He got up and adjusted his cock. He'd been hard since he'd smelled her. Knowing that he wasn't going to touch her again did little to his frame of mind. She was up there, and she was naked. He had told Sally that she wasn't to let her wear any more of Marc's shirts and had given her his. He had gotten all the way downstairs before he realized what he'd done.

"Mother fuck." Khan stood up and began pacing the room. He was so fucked right now he didn't know what to do. He glared again and wondered, not for the first time since entering the bedroom, if Caitlynne had anything to do with this.

He knew that she hadn't, but he wanted to blame someone. The woman upstairs was his mate and she was a fucking human. He paced more until he saw his reflection in the door glass. He looked manic.

Not only that, but his cat was showing. His eyes had darkened and his body mass had expanded. Taking deep breaths in his nose and out his mouth had him calm a little, but a quick trip to the bathroom had him combing his hair and tossing cold water on his face. He looked at the man staring back at him.

"You're so fucked right now you'll never be able to get her away fast enough." The man seemed to mock him, and Khan splashed water at his reflection. He stood there for several seconds wondering if he could jerk off and give his cock some relief, but knew it wouldn't help. He needed the woman.

When he came out, Sally was standing in the kitchen. She looked slightly afraid of him and he tried smiling at her. He didn't think he'd done any good when she backed up. He sat down and tried to calm them both.

"She frightened me. When you called, I thought it was Caitlynne and she'd fallen and hurt the baby." Sally nodded. "Then when I saw the stranger, I was so relieved that I got a little pissed at her for scaring you."

"It's Miss Monica. She was hurt early this morning at work. Mr. Marc brought her here so no one would hurt her again. I think it was her husband who beat her." Khan nodded. That sounded like something that Marc would do. Protect someone.

"I didn't mean to scare you. Or her." He looked up again. "Is she all right? Does she need anything?"

"No. I helped her to dress, and she cried herself to sleep. That other man, her husband, he hurt her badly, Mr. Khan. No woman should have to be afraid of a man who said he'd love her for the rest of her life." She handed him another shirt and he pulled it on. "You frightened her too. You should learn to control your temper around her. She will not take it."

He had a feeling that Sally was right. Miss Monica didn't strike him as the type to sit back and let people scream at her. Or talk to her like she was a small child. But it was going to be a moot point when he had her leave. And she was going to leave.

After he left Marc's house, he went to find him. The construction site was near his house, so he simply walked this time. By the time he got there and saw his brothers, he had nearly convinced himself that she wasn't his mate and that he had made a mistake. Yeah, and monkeys could fly.

"I just left your house," he told Marc after they shook hands. "I think maybe I might have scared Sally. I just wanted you to know." He couldn't do it. He had planned to tell him that he was sending his guest to their parents' house, but didn't because he could see Caitlynne across the way. He turned to leave when Marc stopped him.

"She called me."

Khan wanted to pretend that he had no idea who he meant, but Marc knew better.

"Sally said she had called you when my phone was turned off a little while ago. She told me what happened between you and Monica."

"Nothing happened between us. She was in distress and I helped her to the bed." Reed came toward them and Khan realized that he'd been a little loud. "I picked her up out of the shower and put her into the bed. Nothing else."

"And you wouldn't let her wear my shirt."

Khan didn't say anything to Marc's statement. It was true, but he wasn't going to get himself into anything with him right now. He started to walk away when Walker said his name.

"Is it her?"

Khan didn't turn, but shook his head.

"Are you sure? Because you smell like her, and if what you say is true, then you won't mind if Caitlynne and I take her back to Washington with us."

Khan didn't remember moving or that he'd taken Walker to the ground. He was just over him with his hands around his throat. When he realized what he was doing, he let him go and stood up. Backing away from him, he looked at the rest of his brothers.

"I won't claim her. You know how I feel about this and I won't have anything to do with her. None of you can make me either." He flushed when he realized how stupid he sounded. "I'm going home, and I don't want any of you to come near me. Take her with you, I don't give a shit. You can have her."

~~~

Monica woke late. When she looked at the clock, it was just after midnight. Moving slowly so she didn't cry out if she hurt herself, she took herself to the bathroom again and found a new toothbrush and paste on the counter. After brushing her teeth twice, she moved back to the bed. An elderly man sitting in the rocker startled her.

"I'm George Bowen. I'm Marc's dad. How are you feeling?" She told him fine. "Good, that's good. I can have Corrine, that's my wife, bring you up something to eat. She's been up here about ten times every hour since we came over. Got you some more of that stew you ate earlier."

"I don't have to be waited on. If you can tell me where my clothes are, I'd like to get dressed, please."

He nodded toward the little table near the windows. She went there and found her pants had been washed, but the shirt wasn't hers. She looked at him, and he laughed.

"I believe it's one of Khan's. After earlier, we didn't want anyone to get hurt so we dug up one of his that was at the house. We can be a bit possessive when something like this happens."

She nodded, not having a clue what he was talking about or who.

Going back to the bathroom, she found folded in the shirt, a pair of panties, and some socks. She had no idea where they had come from, but they were cleaner than the ones she had on and she hurriedly pulled them on. The shirt like the one she had just taken off was huge, but she didn't have anything else. Finding a brush, she dragged it through her hair and knotted it at the back of her head. She had to find someone to cut it soon or she was going to.

When she came out again, she was exhausted, and happy to see the man had left. She went through the opened door and stood in the hall for several seconds, trying to figure out where to go. She went toward the sounds of people talking and ended up in a brightly lit kitchen.

Walker was there, as was his wife, Caitlynne. Marc and George were standing next to an elderly woman who was giving them both a hard time about something. Two more men she didn't recognize were there as well as a man from earlier today. She nodded to them all and looked at Marc.

"I'm feeling much better now and was wondering if you'd take me to my apartment? The landlord said he had some of my things, and once I get them, I can head on out." He glanced at the man. "I can make payments to you for what you've done for me. And to you, Walker."

"That won't be necessary." Marc shoved his elbow in the man. "Monica, these are my brothers. This is Reed and Sebastian, and this is my mother Corrine. You've met Caitlynne and Walker, and now my dad. This man, the man from today, is my brother, Khan. He's very sorry for what he did to you today."

"I might have overreacted. I really would like to go now, please." She looked at them all when they seemed to as one look at Khan. "Is there a problem?"

"You might say that." Caitlynne stood up and came toward her as she spoke. "They're all idiots. Come on. Corrine has some soup for you. These guys were just leaving. Unless you have something to say, Khan, you can leave as well."

He looked as if there was plenty to say, but he only shook his head. When the others walked by her, they either tipped their heads or smiled at her. She felt like she was missing something and when Khan turned to look at her, she turned away from him. She had to keep telling herself he didn't want her.

The soup was warm and very good. When Walker came in and asked to see her eyes, she let him. She noticed that he was careful not to touch her. Not even when she started to stagger when he asked her to stand up. When he asked her to wait a few minutes before walking, she looked over at Caitlynne and Corrine. She wasn't sure, but she could swear the two of them were conversing. After Walker left the room, she continued to stand.

"I need to be taken back to my place, please. I'm not sure what's going on here, but something is." Corrine nodded and looked at Caitlynne. "I'm hurt, not stupid, so tell me."

"You're not going anywhere."

She turned to look at Khan.

"You're either going to my house or my parents' house. I'd prefer if you went to theirs, but—"

"I'm not going to either place. I'm going where I want, with or without your permission." He came toward her and she stood her ground. "You're a bully and I don't like you."

"Well, it matters very little what your feelings are, I guess. As of now, and until you heal enough to be on your own, I'm your boss. Now sit down before you fall."

She looked around and noticed that both women were gone.

"I said to sit."

Monica had had enough of him. Striding toward him, she poked him in the chest as she backed him to the wall, and she yelled. She hated yelling, but this man had gotten on her last nerve. "Listen here, you overgrown spoiled child, I will not be ordered about like I'm a small child or some dog you hate. I'm a person, a real, live, living person who has a brain and knows how to use it." She stopped when he did, knowing he couldn't go any further. "You are not my boss, you are not my master, and I will not put up with you acting like you are. I am leaving this house right now, and when I do, if you come near me, talk to me, or so much as glance in my direction, I will buy me a gun and shoot you."

When he didn't move, she growled low. Something she'd not done since she was a child. She'd learned how to do if from the neighbor's cat. Her mother had hated it, and she had broken herself of it so as not to get sent to her room without supper.

"Are you quite through?"

She looked up at him and could see…humor? It was sparkling in his eyes. Instead of answering him, she turned on her heel and moved toward the door. She was nearly there when he grabbed her from behind.

She hadn't meant to cry out. But he'd touched her ribs where they had been broken and she couldn't help it. The room filled with people immediately, and she could hardly breathe. When one of them yelled at Khan to let her go, someone else said to get her outside. She was suddenly in Khan's arms and out in the cold.

"Breathe," he kept saying.

She looked up at him and tried. When he said it four more times, she snapped at him. "I'm fucking trying. Will you stop ordering me around?" She heard laughter and glanced up to see Walker. "I hurt."

"I know, honey. You'll need to be brought back in now and I'll see if you injured anything else. I would say that you didn't, but I don't want to take a chance."

Khan held her as he carried her up the stairs. She tried not to touch him, but she had never been carried like this before and thought it was kind of nice. When he put her on the bed, she noticed that it had been made and everything was put back into order. Not that she'd made a mess, but she had left a towel on the floor, unable to bend to pick it up.

"Put her there, Khan." He laid her gently on the bed as Walker had directed. "I've got it now if you want to go back—"

"I'm not leaving. You can try to make me, but I'm not going anywhere." He looked around the room before looking at his brother again. "I can't. Not with you in here."

Walker nodded and came toward her. When he started to lift her shirt, she heard a low growl. Both she and Walker looked at Khan.

"I'm sorry. I can do this. I know you're trying to help her."

Monica hurt too badly to try and figure it out.

"I'm going to give you something for the pain. You'll feel warm for a few seconds then you won't hurt. I'm doing this so that you don't cry out. I know you don't understand right now, but if you hurt, he's going to try and kill me." She nodded at Walker just before she felt a small pinch in her arm. "Close your eyes, Monica, and let it take you."

Monica tried to open her eyes, and they felt like they'd been glued shut. She had a feeling of coming out from a long tunnel, and every so few inches, she stepped in something sticky. When she finally managed to get them open, she shut them again quickly.

The arm lying across her chest scared her. It was a male arm she knew because a woman would look ridiculous with one as massive as this one. Then she was giggling when she pictured a woman like that in her mind. But sobered quickly when the man attached to the am sat up and looked down at her.

"How are you this morning?" Khan sounded like sex and sleep. She moved her thighs together when she felt warmth gather there. "Don't do that."

She tried to pull away from him, but he held her. "Don't do what?"

"Don't try to hide your scent from me. I like the way you smell. Especially when you're aroused like you are."

She jerked away from him only to remember her ribs.

"Be still. Do you want to be injured forever?"

His voice had gone from soft and sexy to hard and commanding in a second. Before she could tell him she wanted to get up, he rolled to the side of the bed and sat there with his back to her. When he didn't move right away, she started to get up on her side only to realize she was naked again.

"Where are my things? I need my…who undressed me?" She saw the flush on his face and knew that he'd done it. "You pervert. I suppose you had sex with me too. Well, I'd better not catch anything from you. And don't think I know what you—"

"I didn't have sex with you." He stood up and turned his own naked body, hard and huge. "Do you think I'd still be this hard had I entered you in any way?"

She swallowed twice and tried to take her eyes off his cock. He was hard and long and thick. She licked her lips once and looked up at him when he groaned. He looked to be in a great deal of pain.

"I would like nothing more than to bury myself inside of you. Not that I have any intentions of doing so, but if I did have sex with you, you'd not have to wonder in the morning if we did." He stroked his cock twice and looked down at her. "For that matter, I'd probably be buried in you before you woke, screaming out my name."

He moved around the bed, and when she thought he was going to make good on his threat, he went into the bathroom and slammed the door. She heard the shower turn on and thought of joining him there when she realized what she was doing.

Getting out of bed, she moved toward one of the dressers and opened a drawer at random. Taking out the first thing she touched, she pulled the t-shirt over her head and grabbed up a pair of boxers. She hurt like hell, but she wasn't staying in this house another minute. As soon as she stepped out of the door, she realized that this was not the same house.

Moving down the stairs, she was opening the kitchen door when someone was pulling into the driveway. Flagging them down, she saw it was Corrine.

"I want you to take me to town. I don't have any money, but I won't stay with that lunatic another moment."

She looked at the house then back at her before nodding.

"Thank you."

Once she was in the car, she noticed that she didn't have any shoes on and she had no idea where she had left them. Corrine turned the heat up and kept glancing at her, but didn't say anything. By the time they were pulling in front of yet another strange house, Monica knew she was never getting away from these people. But Corrine spoke before she could tell her she was calling the police.

"I'll have George take you into town. I'm stopping here to get you something more to wear." She got out, came around to her side, and opened the door. "He won't know you're here until you're gone if we hurry."

She did hurry. And was sitting in a hotel room forty minutes later with her things from her apartment as well as fifty dollars from George. Lying back on the bed, Monica burst into tears. She couldn't take much more of this.

Kathi S. Barton

40

Chapter Four

"What do you mean you won't tell me where she's at? I want you to tell me right now." Khan paced the spacious kitchen while he waited for one of his parents to tell him what they'd done with Monica.

"I told you that you don't deserve to know. When I pulled up to the house to check on her and she came flying out…she didn't even have any shoes on. Not even a coat. It's nineteen degrees outside. What if I hadn't come when I did? Would she still be out dressed like that? She'd be dead." His mom wiped at the tears that had been flowing since he stormed in the house over an hour ago.

He'd come out of the bathroom ready to talk to her. He'd taken a cold shower and had jerked off twice, trying to get the sight of her naked and under him out of his mind. But it had done nothing but frustrate him more. He made a decision that he'd fuck her, but not come inside of her, nor bite her. He had to or he'd never let her go. He started pacing again when he felt his cock jerk in his pants.

"Son," his dad started, and he looked at him. "You've made it perfectly clear that you don't want her, and when you hang around with her, it's only going to make it harder on you."

Khan didn't think his cock could get any harder. "I need to make sure she's all right." His dad was already shaking his head at him. "Dad, I can't be a mate to her. She's married and human."

"No, she's not."

He looked up at his mom.

"She's not married. And the man who beat her is a stalker, not even her boyfriend according to Caitlynne. He's run her out of other towns by going to her place of business and trashing her apartment. The poor girl does not need you sniffing around her if all you want is a good screw."

Khan felt his face heat up. His mother had been getting more and more blunt all the time and he blamed it on Caitlynne. She was a bad influence to her. He started to tell his mom he did not want only a good screw when he had a sudden vision of him looking up at Monica's face while he drank from her body. He was in major trouble here.

"It doesn't matter. You're to stay away from her."

He glanced at his dad and wanted to tell him to fuck off. But he'd seen that look before. As a child when he'd been disobedient. He didn't remember what he'd done, but did remember the trip to the shed. He hadn't been able to sit down for a few days.

"I'll find her on my own." He stood up and went to the door. "I want you to stay out of this. Please. I have to explain why we can't be mates and show her that I'm not out of my mind."

He was pretty sure he was for even thinking about this, but went out into the afternoon cold. She was out there somewhere and he didn't have a clue. He looked toward Reed's house and saw his car parked in the drive. He started there, knowing that Reed could do his computer magic and find her for him. Khan was smiling by the time he was knocking on the door.

They couldn't make him do anything he didn't want any more. And he wanted to talk to Monica. He wasn't going to have sex with her, but there was no reason he couldn't have a long talk with her. He just hoped that she'd not made good on her promise to get a gun just yet.

Reed was helpful to a point. He wasn't thrilled about helping him until he promised to not tell Mom his secret. He had a job. A very good job and was working with Caitlynne on some very high profile cases. But he couldn't get his desk in the house and needed help building it.

It took them nearly three hours and a case of beer to bring in the heavy boxes and put the sucker together. It might not have taken quite that long had they not gotten sidetracked talking about the current case.

"There are supposed to be bodies all over this property, but with the equipment they're using, I can't track it on my computer. It's not compatible. And since I'm not allowed to go out on sites with them, I have to rely on the information they send me."

"Where is this place?" Reed told him where it was. "That's within flying distance. Why don't you just fly out there, shift, and have a look around."

That had been the perfect solution for his brother, but not for him. There wasn't anyone registered in any of the local hotels by her name. While Khan was pulling on his coat to leave, Reed yelled that he'd found her.

"I just searched for check-in times. You told me when she left your place and when you got to Mom and Dad's. It had to be within minutes of you getting there because Dad pulled in when you did. So she had to be close. So I found her under the name Preston Monte. I think her last name is Preston."

More than Khan knew. He got into his truck and started for the hotel. He had no idea what he was going to say to her once he saw her, but he wanted to clear the air. He may not want her as a mate, but she didn't have to think he was a bastard either. He pulled up in front of the hotel just as someone was peeling out. He ran to the door she was supposed to be in. It was standing ajar.

"I've called the police. And they said they'd be right here. I mean it. If you don't get out of here, I swear to you I'm going to hunt you down and kill you."

Khan looked back at the open door then at the bathroom door where her voice was coming from. It was the prick that hurt her. And he'd found her again. Khan walked to the door and knocked. She screamed and it was everything he could do not to break it down again and save her.

"It's me. Khan Bowen. He's gone." She didn't make any more threats, for which he was grateful. "Are you hurt? Did he hurt you?"

"What do you want?"

Fair enough question, he supposed, and he turned when someone stood at the door.

"I heard her scream. I have my children to think of, so she has to leave here now. I don't want to have to call the cops." The woman had a ball bat in her hand and looked out at the lot. "That other man, you know who he was?"

"No, ma'am. But I'll take care of any damages he did. And Miss Preston is going to come home with me. I'll make sure she's all right." The door behind him opened, and he turned to Monica. She looked terrified and pissed.

"I'm all right now. Thank you. I'll be on my way as soon as this man leaves."

He didn't say anything, but nodded to the woman.

As soon as she shut the door, Khan pulled Monica into his arms and held her. When she started shaking, he picked her up and held her while she cried. Her sobbing made him hurt in more ways than he could imagine. But he didn't let her go even when she struggled against him.

"Why do you keep showing up and dragging me to you only to push me away? I'm not a yo-yo, you know." He let her go, but when she moved toward the door, he didn't move. "I would very much like for you to go. I have to…I have to find somewhere to go."

"Come back to my place with me and I'll take care of you. I'm not particularly fond of doing it, but you are my responsibility. So gather what you need and we'll be on our way." He leaned back in his chair and waited for her to do as he'd told her to.

~~~

Monica closed her mouth with a snap. He actually thought that she would simply do as he told her after that comment. She waited for a full minute to see if he would tell her he was kidding, and when he didn't, she moved to the bed and picked up her few things. Including the cell phone George had given her just in case.

Going to the bathroom, she turned on the shower. She didn't want one, but it would cover the noise of what she was really doing. The window had opened easily enough earlier when she thought she was going to have to leave that way. Tony had forced his way into her little area, and she'd barely made it to the bathroom and locked the door before he came in. She tossed her bag out the window and then stood on the toilet.

Moving out the window hurt, but she was suddenly on the other side. Picking up her bag, she moved down the alley and behind two buildings. Every few minutes, she would look to

45

see if Khan was following her, and when she was able to slip into a vacant building, she pulled out the cell phone and dialed the first number she came to. Unfortunately, it wasn't George. But she thought maybe Caitlynne would help her anyway.

"I don't know if you remember me, but I'm Monica Preston. Your husband helped Marc when I was hurt." She wasn't assured by the laughter, but decided she might be her only hope. "That Neanderthal man that claims to be related to Marc has ordered me around for the last time."

"What the fuck has he done now?" There was still humor there, but also a bit of steel. "Where are you, Monica? I'll come and beat the ever-loving shit out of him and make him behave. Has he talked to you about anything yet?"

"No. I don't think he knows what the word talk means. He can order just fine, but I don't take them well." She wiped at the useless tears and looked out the window to see if he was coming yet. "I left him in that hotel that your father-in-law took me to this morning. The landlady said I can't go back because Tony showed up and tried to get me to go with him. Then Khan shows up and tells me that while he's not particularly fond of me or his responsibility to me, he'll allow me to stay at his home. I want to kick his nuts up around his ears."

There was silence on the other end, and Monica was sure she'd gone too far. When Caitlynne started talking, she sounded like she was speaking a foreign language; it was full of words that Monica was sure would make a sailor blush. When she finally slowed down, Monica thought maybe that she'd like this woman if they had met under different circumstances. The woman was a lot of fun.

"I'm going to come and find you. I don't suppose you know where you are, do you?"

Monica told her the name of the street she'd been on when she'd entered the building.

"Okay. About four blocks to the south is a restaurant. It's called Mild Pepper. Do you know where that's at?"

"Yes. It's on Sandalwood. I know where it is."

She told her to go there.

"But what about Khan? What if he comes looking for me and finds me there?"

"He'll be coming home soon. I'm going to talk to his dad and tell him what I know. George won't be happy, but he'll help us. I'm going to take you with me, do you have a problem with that?"

She did, but wherever they went, she was pretty sure that neither Tony nor Khan would find her. "No. I don't have a problem with that. I don't have any money, though. Is that going to be a problem for you?"

Caitlynne laughed. "No. I have enough for this trip. You let me handle things here and I'll meet you at the Pepper. If you see Khan, which I highly doubt you will, I want you to find Mr. Shaver. Tell him that I sent you and that you love baseball. Tell him that you love baseball. He'll know what to do. And, Monica?"

"Yes?" She was afraid of what she was going to say, of what she was going to demand of her, and she waited, holding her breath.

"I like you. I think you're going to do just fine." The line went dead and Monica stared at the phone for several seconds before she put it in her pocket. What on earth was that supposed to mean? She had no idea, but made her way out onto the street and headed toward the Pepper.

It took her longer than she thought it would to get there. Her ribs were hurting, but that wasn't all of it. She was afraid she'd be seen. Twice she saw Tony's car, and another time, she thought she saw Khan, but knew at the last second it wasn't him. That man was much shorter and fatter than Khan. But Tony, she knew.

Anthony Barr had been hurting her for nearly two years. The police in her hometown had done nothing to help her. She knew that going to them had been a waste when she found out that Tony was the senator's son. And that everyone was afraid of him.

But Tony had decided that she was his. And after he nearly drove her nuts for two weeks, she went out with him. Hoping that he'd leave her alone afterwards, she tried her best to make it the worst date he'd ever had.

About halfway into their dinner, he reached across the table and hit her. Her head swam with pain, and she stood up to leave him. But he pulled out a gun, put it to her head, and made her finish her dinner.

No one helped her. The waitress that served them never looked at her and continued serving them as if Tony wasn't forcing her to sit there. When it came time for dessert, he asked her politely, even with the gun still to her head, if she wanted some chocolate. He said he knew it was her favorite. While she was shaking her head, he ordered them both coffee and talked to her as if this was a perfectly fine way to dine. After that, things got really bad.

The police told her to let him have his way and when she'd tried to get in to see the senator, Tony was there waiting for her. He had hit her again then and had used one of his father's statues on his desk to beat her. She'd ended up in the hospital where she had run the first time. And she'd been running since.

Monica went into the Pepper and watched from the doorway into the street. Tony drove by, and she nearly bolted, but was stopped when a large man held her back. When she tried to peel his fingers off her arm, he told her that he was Shaver and that Caitlynne had told him to watch for her.

"Which one of them hurt you like this?" His voice left her no doubt that he was pissed off. "You say his name and he's as good as dead. Nobody hits a woman and lives to tell about it when I'm around."

"No. You can't. His father, he's really important, and he won't help me anyway." She was babbling and turned toward the street again. "No one will help me get away from him."

Caitlynne walked in, said her name, and Monica turned to see her. The woman was simply the most beautiful person she'd ever seen. When she told her that she was parked in the back, she went with her. Mr. Shaver handed Caitlynne a large bag of what smelled like heaven and spoke in low tones to her. As soon as she nodded, Caitlynne came toward her and helped her into the big truck. Soon they were flying down the highway.

"Walker is staying behind for a couple of days, but I have to go back to DC. That's where you and I are headed. Once we're there, we'll get you some clothes and some medications to make—"

"Thank you for helping me, but I can't afford clothes or medications. I don't have any money other than the fifty dollars that George gave me. I know I said I'd be fine going with you, but you don't know what kind of person the man who's chasing me is, and Khan is your relative. I think if you would just drop me off near the bus station, I can make it somewhere on my own."

She didn't say anything for several minutes. Her phone rang twice, but she ignored it and drove on. When she did finally say something, Monica wasn't sure if she should believe her or not.

"I work for the CIA. Actually, I run it. I have some very powerful people, the president for one, in my corner. If this man fucks with you, he fucks with me, and I don't like to be fucked with. Understand?"

"No. No, I don't. You run the CIA and tell me you have the president on speed dial." Caitlynne snorted. "Okay, you might not have him on speed dial, but it doesn't matter. That man is a danger zone, and when he finds me, I'm either going to be killed by him or kill him myself. I'm so sick of running all the time."

"Good for you." Then she smiled at her. "But you're going to Washington with me."

Chapter Five

Tony looked everywhere for Monica. She was out there somewhere and needed him and he couldn't find her. Driving again past the last place he thought he'd seen her, he nearly had an accident thinking he'd seen her go into a restaurant. By the time he parked and went inside, she'd disappeared again. And the people inside were of no use to him. He didn't even know why those types of people, foreigners, were allowed to work in this country.

Going back out to his car, he stopped on the street and looked. Nothing. He wished now he had simply broken down the door to her hotel room and made her see reason and come back with him. The girl just needed a little more help in understanding that he was trying to help her.

He had been looking for her for a month now. He tried to remember the last time he'd seen her or talked to her before this morning and all he could recall was that she'd been defiant again. Sassed him as well. He'd only hit her to show her that she needed to have respect for her betters, and that when he told her to do something, she should simply give him what he wanted. Like everyone else did.

Tony stopped at the hotel he'd found her in and watched a big man come out of the room. He didn't look like anyone he'd ever met before and wondered what he was doing in his fiancé's room. He was just pulling into the lot of the hotel again when the man got into his truck and left. Tony stared after the man for several seconds before he realized he should have gotten the license plate and had his daddy run it for him.

And following him was out of the question. He'd been going in the opposite direction of where his own hotel was, and he didn't feel like driving any more tonight. So Tony got back into his car and went back to his room in the Hamilton Hotel. He'd had to push his weight around there as well. But they knew who was in charge and had even told him the first night was free. Tony had called his dad to get that little favor taken care of, but he didn't care. What the hell was his daddy good for if not helping his only son out once in a while?

The room had been cleaned from his stay the night before. He laid on the bed and thought about the girls he'd had brought up, as well as the coke his buddy Steve had hooked him up with. It had been one hell of a party. And he thought maybe he'd try to top it tonight. His phone ringing had him rolling over and reaching for the bedside table.

"What are you doing down there, Anthony? Do you have any idea how much extra it costs us when you trash a room like you did that one?" His mother was not his favorite person. "I want you to come home this minute. This obsession with this girl has gotten out of hand."

"I love her. And I'm going to marry her. She just needs to learn to listen." He looked at the bruise on his hand as he continued. "You said you liked her when I told you about her."

"I most certainly did not. I told you to fuck her and get her out of your system. But now you've gone beyond what we can cover up by chasing her across three states and hurting her every time. She keeps running away. Why don't you get it through your sick mind that she doesn't want anything to do with you?"

His head pounded when she yelled at him like this. He put the phone on the bed and began beating his fists against his forehead to make her stop. Over and over she yelled at him, and he couldn't take it any longer. He didn't even know why she thought she had any say in what he did any longer. She and his father were divorced and had been for nearly three years.

Picking up the phone again, he tried for calmness. "Mother, I want you to stop calling me if you don't have anything good to say. I love this one, and I'm going to make it work this time. You'll see. Once she learns her place, we'll be able to live happily ever after, and you'll come to love her as I do."

When she started talking again, he leaned over and hung up the phone. When it rang almost immediately, he put a pillow over his head and tried to block it out. When that didn't work, he got up and left his room. She had done this. Driven a stake through his relationship with his mother. Now he had to go home and fix this.

He drove all night, only stopping for gas. Tony was near her home nearly thirty hours later and pulled into the next street to wait. He knew that on Wednesdays his father came to visit her and he wondered what day of the week it was. Pulling out his cell phone, he realized it was Wednesday and was excited. He was going to get to see them both and have a little talk with them. Closing his eyes, he leaned back on the seat and waited.

He woke around dusk and drove to his mother's home. He didn't see his father's car in the drive and thought he'd missed him. Just as he was about to turn the corner to simply go in and have a little talk with mother dear, he saw his dad pull in. He completed the circle and came back around to park across the street from them.

He walked up the sidewalk and knew just how this conversation was going to go. She was going to yell and his dad was going to tell her to calm down. After a few tears, they would try to tell him that this girl was like the others and that they didn't want to have to take care of another family. He would tell them she had none, that he'd already thought of that. He slipped his key in the door and tried to turn it.

She'd changed the locks on him. Tony stepped back and tried to see in the windows, but all he was able to see was a distorted view of the furniture he knew lay beyond. Instead of knocking, because he knew where they'd be, he went around the back of the house and walked up to the glass doors that led into the summer room. Pulling out his knife, he slit the screen, then punched a hole in the glass. Reaching in, he unlocked the door and stepped inside.

The stereo was on full blast with music that made his head pound. Going through the house, he picked up two things from the kitchen and made his way to the living room where they both were. His mom was sitting with her back to him, and his father was sitting in the chair to her left. They were both holding a glass of wine. There was a tray of cheese and crackers and a bowl of fruit.

As a child, he'd wanted to eat in front of the fireplace, but they'd never let him. He'd tried once to have a cookout in here, roasting marshmallows in the fireplace until he'd gotten tired, but someone hadn't come to check on him soon enough and the carpet had caught fire. When he'd gotten burned, a scar he held today, he had hated any sort of fire near him. He glanced down at the quarter-sized scar and sneered at it.

Walking up behind his mother, he yanked back her head and sliced open her throat with the knife he'd picked up in the kitchen. When she made a noise, his father jumped up from his chair and started for him. Tony stabbed him in the chest with the corkscrew.

Dropping the knife he'd used on his mother, he went around the couch and toward his father. Reaching blindly for the things on the fireplace, he grabbed up the poker there and hit his father in the head. Liking the sound it made, he continued hitting him until his arm hurt. Dropping it on the floor, he sat down in his father's chair. Taking the cheese and crackers, he tossed off the ones covered in blood and finished off the food. He didn't care for the fruit, but ate what was blood free and then sat back in the chair.

"I tried to tell you. I did. I said if you didn't let me have my way, I would make you pay. Both of you." He kicked out at his father. "And what are you doing here in the first place? I've told you several times that I didn't want you seeing her, that she was bad for me, and here you are." He laughed.

Yes, he thought, here they were. Both of them paid for making him upset. Tony realized he was getting the chair dirty and stood up. He knew that the cleaning person would be upset with him so he took off his shoes and carried them up to the bathroom.

He had clothes here, he was sure. What kind of mother would toss them out because her only son had moved on? Besides, he'd told he not to do it, and most of the time, she listened. This time, he was glad that she had.

Getting out of the shower, he dried off and put on the clean clothes. Putting his dirty ones in the hamper, he wondered if they would ever be clean again. He went down the hall to his mother's room and looked for anything of value. He took all her jewelry, as well as the three grand he'd found in her purse. Tony didn't take the card because the last time he'd done that, she'd simply canceled them. It had been embarrassing and a waste of her time.

His father had a room here too, but he didn't find anything much worth his effort. There was about three hundred dollars in his wallet, and Tony took his car keys as well. He'd never been able to drive it and had decided that he'd take it out for a spin before he left.

Going back out, he started the car and drove it carefully around the house. He didn't want to dent it; it really was a nice car. When he was near the pool, he got out and uncovered it before he went back to it. Leaving the door open, he gunned the engine and rolled out as it splashed into the pool. He closed the cover back over it and went to his own car. Going back, he locked up the house again and left.

Tony was nearly an hour away when he realized they'd never gotten around to talking about Monica. He'd meant to tell his mother that he wanted her to have a big wedding with all the trimmings. Next time, he decided; the next time he came for a visit, he'd speak to them about it.

~~~

By the time they landed in DC, Monica had decided that this was the smartest move she'd ever made. The jet was lovely, and she'd been served champagne in a fluted glass while eating the goodies from the Mild Pepper. Some of the things she'd only wanted to try, but had never been able to afford before.

"How much do I owe you? I don't have much, but I always pay people back." She pulled out her notebook and showed it to Caitlynne. "I can't make much of a payment, but as soon as I get one of these paid off, I'll be able to pay more."

"How long do you think you can keep this up?" Caitlynne had showed her around the massive house and they had settled in the living room with a roaring fire. "I mean, it's all well and good that you pay your bills, but if this guy keeps this up, you'll be dead, and who will pay them for you?"

"I don't know." She put her things back in her bag. "I do know that I'm not a freeloader and that I pay my way when I can. And I never asked for him to do this to me. I've been trying to get someone to listen to me about this for months."

"I'll listen to you. And believe it or not, I want to help you. Tell me, who he is? Tell me who he is and where he lives and I'll make sure he doesn't hurt you again." Caitlynne sat up in her chair and looked her right in the eye. "Tell me."

Monica got up to pace. She didn't touch any of the pretty things, but she did so want to. There were pine cones in a glass jar and pretty shells lying in a row from large to the smallest one. When she saw a picture of Caitlynne and Walker together with the rest of the Bowens, her heart twisted a little.

"His dad is something of a big deal in this area. The last time I was here, he was mayor. I think he's moved up from there since then. His mom, someone I'd met once, has parties that people like me only get to serve at." She didn't bother turning when Caitlynne spoke.

"So you're from here. I thought that you lived in Rhode Island." Monica looked at her then. "I've done some research on you. I couldn't be in the position I'm in without taking precautions."

Monica nodded. "I'm from here. Rhode Island is where my father lived. My parents were divorced. My mother...I don't have any proof, but I know that Tony killed her and my dad. He was...is obsessed with having me under his control."

"Tony who?"

Monica knew that eventually she'd have to tell her, but skipped answering her for now. She ran her finger down a picture that had who she thought was Caitlynne as a child. She'd looked so sad.

"I first met him when I was serving at a function his parents were giving. I didn't do anything to try and attract his attention, but he seemed to be everywhere I was. When I went out to my car to leave, he was there. He told me that he'd had someone tell him which one it was." Monica stared out the window that looked out over a lovely park and knew for some reason that it was her yard and not a park at all. "When he…after he hurt me that night for telling him that I could drive home, he stalked me for weeks until I gave in and went out with him. It ended with him holding a gun to my head and making me eat with him. I even went to his father and he told me that it would be better for all of us if I simply gave Tony what he wanted. His father offered to pay me well to let him do what he wanted until he tired of me."

"Christ." Caitlynne didn't ask again, for which Monica was grateful for. "When did you figure out he might have killed your parents?"

"He told me. He said that as long as I had them, I couldn't love him properly. He even told me how he'd done it." She shivered and watched a bird dance along the snow. "They hadn't done anything wrong to him. Neither had I. He simply wanted them gone, and he killed them."

Her phone rang and when Caitlynne didn't answer it, Monica asked her if she wanted her to step out. She shook her head and asked her to come and sit down. She did, fully expecting Caitlynne to tell her that she didn't believe a word she was saying and that she was turning her over to the police. Before she did that, she wanted Caitlynne to know who he was.

"His name is Anthony Barr. His parents are Anthony Senior and Claudine Barr. I know where the mother lives, but not the dad." When Caitlynne didn't move, Monica stood up. "I know that you don't believe me. I don't blame you. I wouldn't either if I heard this story, but I would ask that you don't tell anyone where I am."

"Sit down. Please." Caitlynne finally picked up her phone and answered it this time. "I need you to come here now. Yes, I know what time it is. It's time for you to get your ass over here like I told you. And bring your toys. We've got some things to look into."

Monica looked at the door and wondered if she could make it. But Caitlynne spoke again, and she was suddenly very afraid.

"That was a friend of mine who has been looking into the deaths of a few women in this area. He's been doing it for a few years now and he may need your help. He's told me for years that it was the Barr boy and that his parents knew about it all along." Caitlynne stood up, guided her to the couch, and pushed her down. "I'm going to call my husband, and you're going to sit right there until Marshall comes here and talks to you. If you leave, I'll call Khan, tell him where you are, and tie you up until he gets here. You might be surprised to know that as much as I dislike his tactics, I think you should tell him everything you've told me."

"I can't. What if they come here? What if they bring Tony with them when they come? I can't let anyone hurt him." Monica flushed when she realized what she'd said. "These people have money and they're not afraid to toss it around to get what they want."

She grabbed her bag and reached into her wallet. When she found what she was looking for, she shoved it at Caitlynne. It was the check that Mr. Barr had written her several months ago when she'd told him she was going to the police.

"See what they do? They write checks and think that's enough. They think that everyone has a price because they do." She pressed the check, dirty money, as far as she was concerned, into her hand. "I don't have a price and I won't let them try to buy me off. Not even if it means I have to run for the rest of my life."

She started blindly for the door and was stopped when Caitlynne stepped in front of her. When she tried to get out of her way as easily as she could, the woman simply put her arms around her and held her. Monica cried as she was led back to the couch. Caitlynne didn't pull away after she had her there, but continued to hold her. When Monica was cried out, she pulled away, but didn't leave.

"I'm not usually such a cry baby." She smiled at her. "I've had a shitty few years. I'm so sorry. I didn't mean to unload on you and get you all wet."

"Don't concern yourself with it. Marshall will be here soon and when he is, we'll be able to figure this out. And once we do, I'd like for you to talk to Khan. He's in a state not knowing where you are."

Monica said she'd think about it. She didn't think that the man was stable and told her so. After Caitlynne roared with laughter, she got up to make them something to eat, or so she said. Ordering in was apparently what she did best. She ordered them Chinese.

Caitlynne also said, "And for the record, Khan has been hurt as well. Not nearly as badly as you have been, or as physically, but she did nearly destroy him. He might be able to help in ways you can't imagine."

When Marshall showed up, he had someone with him. She tried not to stare, but the man looked just like the president. The President of the United States. And when Caitlynne called him Warren, Monica knew it was him.

"It's me, and thank you for noticing." He winked at her. "I get no respect from that one and it matters little to her that I got her the job she currently has."

"Blow me, asshole."

Monica looked at the two men and back at Caitlynne when she told the president he was a prick. This was just too surreal.

Chapter Six

Khan sat on the plane and tried not to look at his brothers. He'd been in a fight with one or more of them since his dad had ordered him home the day before yesterday. And now he was finally going to get to see Monica. And from what Caitlynne had said to him last night, and she'd said plenty, Monica wasn't going to take his shit any longer.

"You tell her. Everything, or so help me, I will. And if I do, I'll make sure you never find her ass. And you know I can do it too." She paused for breath, and he started to tell her what she could do with her bad self when she continued. "And, Khan, you should know something else. Tony, the man who is after her, is right here in Washington."

That shut him up. He asked her what he needed to do. She didn't speak for several seconds, and he knew she was crying.

"I don't know, Khan. I really like this girl. I know that I teased you about finding someone and her being more than you can handle, but..." She sniffled. "This girl is almost more than I can handle. She's had her parents murdered and so much done to her, yet she continues on. How does she do it?"

"I'll fix this. I swear to you, I'll fix this." She said he'd better. "Caitlynne, please don't keep her from me any longer.

I need to see her. I was…I treated her badly. I treated her like… Walker said I treated her like an animal."

"You ordered her around like she was. What did you expect her to do, Khan? Jump when you said to? Roll over when you needed to fuck her? She isn't going to roll over for anyone, least of all you."

He'd figured that out when he'd broken down the bathroom door and found her gone. There was blood on the window she'd climbed out of. And when he'd looked down, he was surprised at how far she'd dropped to get away from him. Because that was what she'd done, she'd run away from him.

When they were told they were about to land, he looked over at Walker. He hadn't spoken to him in hours and if he was going to be staying at his house, he wanted it to be better than this. Plus, he was pretty sure he was going to need his help explaining to Monica what he was.

"I'm sorry." Walker looked at him then away. "I truly am, Walker. Not just for upsetting your mate, but for the past few years. I've been…"

"An ass? A prick? Maybe even a dumbass?" Walker didn't smile and Khan knew he wasn't kidding. "You made her cry. Do you know how hard it was for me not to find you and rip your fucking throat out? How hard it is for me still not to do it?"

Khan shivered because he knew that fucking with another's mate would get you killed whatever your status was in the family. He nodded, knowing that anything he said now would be nothing compared to the pain he'd caused him, caused them both.

"Caitlynne said you're going to fix this with Monica. You have any plans other than ordering her to believe you? I'm not sure, but I don't think that's going to work with her any longer. She's been through a lot."

And most of it was because of him. Especially lately, he'd been an overbearing prick, but he was going to show her he could help her. He got off the plane with the others and told them he needed to make a couple of stops. There was a limo there to pick them up and take them to the house. Khan said he would take a cab.

"I'll go with you. The others can go ahead." Walker told the driver to come back for them. "We'll have some lunch too."

The first stop he made was at a florist. He was standing there looking at all the different colors and kinds and realized he knew very little about his mate. He looked at Walker when he touched his arm.

"Overwhelmed?"

Khan nodded.

"Me too, sometimes. Caitlynne isn't like most women. She carries a gun, kills the bad guys, and is around more men in one day that most women are in a lifetime. It's difficult to be around her when she smells like so many of them."

"How do you do it? How do you let her leave you every day, come back here without you. How do you stand it?" Khan smiled at the grin Walker gave him. This was going to be good.

"I mark her every night."

He ended up getting her lilies. They were pretty and happy-looking to him. He didn't tell Walker or the man helping him that, but ordered her two dozen of them. Then he saw the little violet. He leaned down and looked at the soft, velvety leaves and thought of her skin. The tiny little flowers reminded him of her eyes, the darkest purple he'd ever seen. He asked that one of those to go as well.

They ended up having a quick lunch and went to the mall. This place was huge. After making several stops they called for the limo to come back, they had filled the trunk as well as most of the back seats with them. Both he and Walker had bags on their laps as it was. The driver said he'd have them brought in. Khan carried one bag in himself.

She was still asleep when he got there. The maid had informed them that Mr. Marshall and the president had left just after two in the morning and that the young miss had been up when she'd come in and that had been at six this morning. It was just after two in the afternoon.

Khan went to the room where she was and saw that the flowers had been brought in. He picked up the violet, took it to her bedside table, and set it there for her. He put his pink bag on the floor beside her and sat down.

Her face was healing nicely, and the swelling had gone down. He touched his finger to her skin and smiled when he'd been right about the flower he'd gotten her. When she stirred a little, he moved back to the chair to watch her. A few minutes later, she woke.

"Hi. How are you?"

She looked around the room, but didn't say anything.

"I bought you some flowers. I've never bought flowers before."

He sounded lame even to his own ears. When she stretched, he noticed how the shirt she had on cupped her breasts and he looked away. He wasn't here to make love to her, but to beg her to forgive him.

"I have to get up. I want you to go away. And I don't want to argue with you about it either." She pulled the sheet up over her and frowned. "How long have you been here?"

"Not long. I'd like to...I need to speak to you first. If you don't mind. I have some things I have to explain to you."

She snorted. "If you mean you have some orders to dictate to me, then no thanks. I've had enough of you treating me like a subhuman. I'm a real person, just like you are."

Perfect opportunity, he thought. "Not really. I mean, I'm not a real person. Not like you anyway. I'm a bit more."

She cocked her brow at him. "Oh, is that right? You're better than me. Well, how fucking fantastic for you. Then you won't mind if I tell you to stay away from my less than perfect self. Get out."

He'd fucked that up royally. "That's not what I mean. I'm more than you because...I'm not really human."

"I won't argue with you there."

He glared, but tried again. "I'm a panther." There, he'd told her. Not the way he'd planned, but now she knew. He waited for her to ask questions, but all she did was stare at him. Just when he was going to explain what he meant, she spoke.

"I'm pretty sure they disbanded in the eighties. And not a group I would have associated you with. Especially since you don't seem all that political."

It took him several seconds to realize what she'd meant. He supposed it might have been funny had he not been trying his best not to get pissy and to keep her from leaving him. He was pretty sure that laughing right now might get him killed. And not by the woman his brother had married either.

"Not a Black Panther, but a real one. The kind that walks on four paws. My entire family is. Including Caitlynne." He watched her for signs of fear. But she looked...amused.

"Okay. And I suppose, oh, I don't know, the president is a bat and his aide is a dragon. You're insane if you believe that."

"No. It's true, and the president is a white Bengal, as is the aide. But I think he's golden, not white." He stood up and started unbuttoning his shirt. "Would you like to see him?"

~~~

Monica was shaking her head even as he took off his shirt. When he had it off, she expected to see a tattoo or something like that on him, but that was not the case. He took off his belt and unsnapped his jeans. But she stopped him.

"Look, if you want me to believe this, I will. There's no reason for you to do this." She eyed him closely. "Are you your panther now?"

He laughed at her, and she felt foolish. "No. I think you'll know when I shift when I'm him. And, Monica, please don't scream or run. If you do, you'll make him chase you, and he loves to run."

She nodded. When he slipped off his pants, along with his boxers, she had a moment of sheer pleasure run though her body. He was beautiful. When he growled low, she looked up at his face.

"I'm going to show you my cat then, if you still want me, I'll change to human again and make love to you. Is that all right with you?"

She nodded, not sure what else to do. "Good, because I can smell you, and I want nothing more than to come deep inside of you."

And as suddenly as he was naked before her, he was gone. And in his place stood a humongous panther. She scrambled to the top of the bed to get away, and he leapt on the bed with her. She eyed the door and wondered if she could make it when he snarled at her.

"Nice panther. I just want to go and get some help. You stay right here and I'll—" His big paw landed on her leg and she cried out. "Please don't eat me." She looked down at him when he moved closer. He didn't let her go, but he did move a lot slower toward her. Just when she was going to scream, he licked her foot.

"Stop that. What are you doing? Seeing if I'm tender enough for you? Stop that right now."

She thought he was laughing at her. And when he licked her again, she wiggled her toes. It wasn't a bad feeling. His tongue was rough but soft and when he moved up her leg, she stretched out for him.

"Licking is fine, but no biting." She watched him as his tongue lapped the wound on her leg. She nearly jerked away when she realized that it didn't hurt.

"You fixed it." She looked at him. "Can you understand me? What I'm saying to you?" He nodded. "I'm off my rocker here." She looked around the room and saw the flowers. "Are those roses? Did you buy me roses?" He shook his head this time. "It's really you, isn't it? You're really a panther and I'm in bed with you." He nodded and licked her thigh. "Are you going to have sex with me like that?"

He didn't move. And she thought maybe his eyes had darkened. Her body felt his gaze, felt everywhere he was touching her. When he lifted his paw off her leg, he moved it up to her belly and nuzzled at her shirt. Without thought to what he might want or to chew on, she lifted it up and exposed her ribs to him.

"I did that climbing out the window at the hotel. I know it was stupid, but you…the human you had made me mad. I don't want you to treat me that way again." His tongue rolled over her ribs and the scrapes and bruises. They no longer stung. "You're healing me."

When he'd licked the area, she nearly put her shirt back down, but he bumped his head against her breast. She wasn't sure about this part, but unhooked her bra and exposed both breasts to him. He watched her as he flicked his tongue over her nipple, and she moaned. Then when he did the same to the other, she wrapped her fingers in his fur and lifted his head.

"You want me, then you do whatever it is to make you human. I'm on fire for you." She was too. And she was wet as well. When he moved back down her body, he lowered his head to her pussy and inhaled deeply. She shifted on the bed and nearly came when he did it again.

He stood near the bed and became Khan again. His cock was the first thing she noticed because he was incredibly hard and straining from his groin. When she reached for him, he took a step back and took a deep breath.

"I'm going to bite you when we come. I'm going to mark you as mine. All right?"

Was he kidding? She didn't care at this point if he tore her throat out so long as he was inside of her. She nodded.

He lifted her up and took her mouth. Her body was molded to his as he took them back to the bed; his mouth was voracious. His tongue, soft and smooth now, touched deep and tangled with hers over and over. His hands tore at her clothes and she at his flesh.

When he took her nipple into his mouth, she cried out, lifted herself up to him to give her all to him. When his cock was at her entrance, she moved and shifted until she felt his crown fill her. Moving again, she tried to take him all.

He tore his mouth from breast and looked down at her. "I know you're not a virgin, but I'm large and I know this will hurt, but I can't wait. I need to fill you."

"Please. Please, take me." He punched hard into her. She screamed out in pain and held him. When he didn't move, she looked up at him.

"I'm so sorry, but I need to move, baby. I swear to you I'll make it better for you next time, but I need to come inside of you." When he moved again, it was slow and easy. "I'll make it up to you, baby."

She felt her body adjust to his. His cock was thicker than she was used to, but he wasn't hurting her any more. She rolled her hips up to take more of him when he licked along her throat. Every part of her body, including, she was sure, her hair, felt it. Moving her head for him, she felt his teeth as they grazed along her skin. Digging her nails into his back to encourage him to do it, she felt his teeth at her earlobe. All the while he was moving in and out of her slowly, steadily.

"You're going to come when I bite you. Come very hard. I can hardly wait to taste you. Lick my tongue into your pussy and drink you." Her hands moved to his chest, and she flicked her nail over his nipple. "Christ, do that again."

She did and drew blood. But instead of feeling bad for hurting him, she found that she wanted to taste him. Lifting her head, she licked the droplet and then covered her mouth over the tiny wound and suckled.

Her climax tore through her, but before she could throw back her head and scream with it, Khan held her to his chest and took her hard. Then he sank his teeth into her neck.

The climax screamed though her body, taking her up and over a crest so high she saw stars behind her closed lids. Even as he lapped at her skin, and her at his, he pounded into her over and over. Then he stiffened and lifted his head. As he snarled, she looked up and saw her blood on his chin, his teeth, longer than before, stained with it. She took his injured nipple again in her mouth and bit him as hard as she could, and cried out when her mouth filled with his blood. As she swallowed, she knew that something had happened, something neither of them had expected. As the darkness took her, she thought he told her he loved her.

Chapter Seven

Khan covered her up again. He'd been checking her for injuries and that her pulse was still beating since he'd realized she was unconscious. He'd rolled off her and the bed so quickly that he'd tripped in the bag he'd meant to give her and turned his ankle. He'd limped to the bathroom to get her a cold rag when he noticed the blood on his chest.

She'd bitten him. Drawn blood and had drunk it in. He rubbed his hand over the tiny scar that was there and smiled again. He tried hard not to think about what she'd done, but couldn't help feeling like he'd been given a great gift. He checked her pulse again.

He hadn't told anyone what had happened, though he was pretty sure they'd heard them. He hadn't thought of the rest of them in the house when he'd taken her. He looked down at her again and wondered at that moment who had taken whom. He caught himself smiling again and turned to the door when someone knocked.

He opened it a crack, just enough to see his brother, Walker, standing there. "Go away. I don't want to wake her."

He laughed. "I don't think that's going to happen. The way she screamed, I'm pretty sure she's going to be out for a while. You okay?"

He nodded then shook his head. "I don't know. She...Christ, Walker, she bit me. And she drew blood."

"I'm happy for you. She'll be fine. She has your blood now and will be fine. I swear it. Come out here. We've got something to—"

"Khan?"

He turned to her when she said his name, shutting the door in Walker's face. He heard him laughing as he made his way to the bed and her.

"Are you hurt? Did I hurt you too much?" He lifted off the cover again and checked her pulse. "I've been so worried after you slipped away that way. Are you sure you're okay?"

"Yes. How are you?" She ran her finger over the scar and looked up at him. "You heal fast, don't you?"

"Yes. So will you now." He lay down beside her, but didn't get under the covers. "You really all right? I didn't mean to bite you so hard. But you're mine now."

She raised a brow at him. "I don't belong to anyone. I'm my own person. And the sooner you figure that out...what do you mean I'm yours?"

"We're a couple, paired. You and I have had sex and exchanged blood. I guess that makes us belong to each other. But mostly, you belong to me." He grinned. "I'm going to protect you."

"I see. Actually, no, I don't." She got up, and he watched her grab things up as she mumbled. He thought he should tell her that he could hear her, but decided that he might get hurt if he did.

"What are you so upset about? I mean, it's not like you've done that good of a job taking care of yourself up till now. I mean, look what happened to you when I first met you. That guy had beaten you for shit and you didn't fight back."

He knew the moment he'd said it he'd screwed up. Before he could tell her that he hadn't meant it that way, she picked up the vase on the dresser and looked like she was going to throw it at him. When she set it down, he let go of his breath with a whoosh. She went to the door and opened it.

"Get out."

He didn't move, wasn't going to.

"If you don't leave this room right this minute, I'm going to scream for your brothers and tell them…tell them that you hurt me."

"They won't believe you. I can't harm you. It's in our DNA not to harm our mate." She left the door open and came to the bed. He thought she was going to forgive him, but she pulled open the drawer. Suddenly, there was a gun in her hand and she was aiming right at his head.

"It's not in my DNA, and I will hurt you. Now you either get out of here right now or they'll take you away in a body bag." More than the gun she held to his head, he believed her because of her voice. It was low, mean, and full of truth. He moved off the bed and stood up. When he reached for his shirt, she jumped on the bed. "I'm not fucking with you any longer. Get out of here." The gun went off an inch from his head, and he watched her steady hand. She'd do it, he realized. She'd fucking shoot him. When the others spilled into the room, he glared at her.

"This isn't finished. You're my mate and I'm not going to put up with this from you or anyone else."

"Well that's just fucking great with me because I'm not putting up with it either." She didn't even look at the door. "Take him away upright or dead, but get him out of here."

Khan walked to the door and out into the hall. He didn't look to see if they followed him or not, but went down the stairs and toward the kitchen. The man standing in front of him was going to regret trying to stop him if he was thinking he could. Before he touched him, he turned. He looked at the man holding the gun on him, standing just inside the door, and then back at the man in front of the door who now had a gun too.

"We've been told to keep you here. You're to go to the living room and have a seat or we are to restrain you." The man by the outside door spoke again. "I don't want to have to shoot you, Mr. Bowen, but I will if I have to."

He was ready to tell them to go for it when Caitlynne and another man he didn't know came through the door. She didn't look happy, and the man beside her looked livid. He lifted his chin. If she wanted to take him on, then he was more than in the mood for it.

"There have been two murders. Brutal ones. Senator and Mrs. Barr were murdered sometime yesterday in Mrs. Barr's home. Her throat was slit and he was bludgeoned to death with a poker." She came into the room and he noticed then how pale she was. "And I brought her here."

He was confused for several seconds. He didn't know who she was referring to until he remembered that Walker told him the man's name that was stalking Monica. Barr. His parents were dead.

"Did he do it?" She nodded as she fell into a chair. "Do you know if he's aware that Monica is here?"

"I don't know. He might not be, but when he doesn't find her there, he's going to come here. He knows who I am and how I'm related to you. He's going to figure out eventually where she might be. I have to send her away. Somewhere that no one knows where to find her until we find him."

"I'm not going to let you do that." He looked up when one of the men shifted on his feet, but didn't lower his gun. "I can't...she's pissed at me right now and will probably welcome him with open arms over me, but I can't let her go."

"Everyone in the household knows she's pissed at you, Khan. You fucked this up, and now I have to protect her. Go back home. You can't fix what she doesn't want fixed."

He slumped in the opposite chair from her as she continued ripping his heart out.

"You can't learn to shut up, can you? You just had to have the last word, didn't you? Why?"

"I don't know how to be with her." He got up to pace and noticed that the men were gone. "Christ, I don't know what to do. What the fuck am I doing with a mate anyway? I can't please her except in bed and then I hurt her. She said I didn't, but she was out for so long. How is it that I'm such a fucking asshole even when I try to be nice?"

"It's called breathing and thinking before you open your mouth."

Khan looked up at Monica who looked like she'd been crying.

"Why do you feel it's necessary to say whatever is on the tip of your tongue? Can't you just say to yourself, 'will this hurt her feelings?' 'Will this make her want to bash my head in and have her dance in my brains?' It's tempting every time you say something that pisses me off."

"You say stupid shit too." She turned to walk away and he called her back. "Please, I'm going to try, but I'm not going to change overnight."

"And you're not going to change at all if you don't try. I can't have you bullying me, Khan. I've put up with too much as it is. I'm not as un-normal as you are, but I do have feelings. Feelings that get crushed when you treat me this way."

"She hurt me." She turned back to look at him. "When she left me, she hurt me, not by what she did, but because she had hurt all of my family too. I'd failed them because I'd fallen for a human."

"And that is my fault how?" She didn't leave when Caitlynne and the others did, but sat down. "I didn't do anything to you but try to keep out of your hair. You kept bringing me back and pushing me away."

"Yeah, a yo-yo." He wanted to reach for her hand, but was afraid she'd jerk away from him. "But it was more than that with Roseann. She had taken not just our secret, but my dignity and my pride. She'd told me that I was less than a man for not doing as she'd wanted and that…"

"And what? What did she say to you?" She took his hand and he laced his fingers into hers. "Tell me all of it, Khan."

"The first time we had sex…I know now that we never made love. It was the first time we'd had sex that I knew there was something about her that was different. It wasn't like she was a paranormal like me, but something about her mind and heart were different. She was cruel to anyone that she considered lesser than her. She treated her servants with little to no respect, and she treated me…" He let go of her hand to get up and pace. "It was as if she had me around because I was something she wasn't supposed to have. But I was okay with that because I thought I loved her."

"Her parents didn't like you?"

He nodded and then shook his head.

"Then what? They liked you?"

"They liked me because I was able to make Roseann happy for a time, but they didn't want me to marry her. They actually tried to pay me off when I asked for her hand. I was too stupid to realize then that they weren't paying me off so much as they were giving me an out. I should have taken it."

He paced more around the room and then opened the refrigerator. He took out the pitcher of tea and filled two glasses with ice. He poured her one then one for himself as he continued. "I told her what we were. I showed her what I could do and how that I could shift. She asked me so many questions that I should have… No, I had no way of knowing that she was thinking along the lines of what I could get her rather than spending the rest of her life with me." He drained his glass and refilled it. "A week or so later, she comes to the house. She's so excited because she has this amazing idea. She wants us to get married right away. I said yes."

"Then what happened? She wanted to marry you, so she must have felt something."

He looked at her and wondered why he'd never seen the difference in the two of them before.

"Khan?"

"She wanted to get married right away, and she wanted me to convert her to what I was. She thought it would be great if the two of us could run in the woods behind her home and be free to do what we wanted." He sipped his drink this time. "But that's not what she wanted. She wanted me to convert her so that she could kill people. Anyone and everyone who pissed her off, she wanted to kill. She told me that when I explained to her that I couldn't change her, that humans died most of the time, and that I wouldn't take the chance in killing her."

"She didn't believe you, did she?"

He shook his head at Monica's question.

"She didn't, and decided that if I wouldn't do it, she'd get one of my other brothers to do it. She started with Reed. He was barely twenty when she approached him. But he wasn't as stupid as she thought and he turned her away. Then she claimed that he'd raped her. And that he was an animal. He was arrested the next day. When she did that, she came to me and told me that if I did as she asked then she'd drop the charges."

When Monica stood up, he thought she was going to leave him, but she didn't. When she stood before him, she sat on his lap and put her arms around him. He moved his chair back so that he could hold her. When she told him to continue, he did without stopping.

"There was no proof that she had been raped. The test that they had done had shown that she'd not had brutal sex, the kind that she said that Reed had done to her. So she changed her story three more times. First, Reed raped her, then Sebastian had beaten her, and then, finally, I robbed her. All of it was dismissed, so that's when she came to me with proof of what we were. It was video that she'd taken one afternoon while we were out in the woods playing around. She'd told me that she erased it, and like a fool, I believed her."

"What happened to it, the video? I would have remembered seeing it if she had blackmailed you. And I'm pretty sure that a man changing into a panther would have been on some news feed."

He kissed her nose. "Caitlynne found it and destroyed it. I don't know when because I've never asked her, but she said she'd found it when she'd been looking into something else she'd been involved in. Roseann not Caitlynne."

She laid her head on his shoulder and didn't say anything. He wanted to ask her all sorts of questions like, was she leaving him? Would she help him become a better man? Would she please give him another chance? But he didn't ask anything of her. He simply held her. When she did talk, he wanted to go and find Roseann and rip her fucking heart out.

"So you hate me because some other woman hardened your heart and your head to anyone else. You have a family that worries about you, yet you let her continue to triumph over you. You've hidden away the best part of you because someone, a bitch of a someone, hurt you." She looked up at him. "I never really thought of you as a coward."

He started to say he wasn't when he really was. He'd been hiding behind her hurting him for a long time. And because of that hurt, he'd been missing out on a great many things. Like loving the woman in his arms.

Monica stood up. "I have to leave here. That man will figure out where I am and he'll come here and hurt you all." He took her hand to stop her. "Don't do this, Khan. You know I'm right."

"No. Yes, you're right, but you can't leave here." He kissed her hands. "I'm not ordering you to stay, but begging you to. He's here. Barr is right here in Washington. And Caitlynne said that he's murdered his parents."

Kathi S. Barton

Chapter Eight

Caitlynne watched her. Monica hadn't said much since she'd come out of the kitchen with Khan. She wondered what he'd said to her to make her not leave, but whatever it was, she was happy for them. When Khan took her hand again, Monica smiled at him, but even Caitlynne could see she wasn't really paying attention to what was going on. It was time to take it up a notch.

"Monica, tell me how you encouraged him to see you."

Monica looked up at her, but didn't comment.

"I mean, why else would he come across the state to find you and to try and get you to come back with him?"

Khan stood up. "You're barking up the wrong tree, Caitlynne. I would suggest that you back off."

"But don't you see? She had to have done something. Maybe you flirted with him a little. Impressed with his money, maybe?"

"No. I didn't do anything. He asked me out and I went, but he wanted more."

Monica looked panicky. Good, this might work. "But you did date him. You said so yourself." When Khan started for her, Walker stepped in front of him and spoke to him in very low tones. "You went out, how was that?"

"Don't do this. I told you what happened. Isn't that enough?" She stood up too. "I don't want to talk about it. I just want to leave."

"He raped you, didn't he?" Monica didn't move and neither did Khan. "You didn't tell me that part. You told me how he held a gun to your head while you sat in the restaurant with him. You told me how no one would help you, but you didn't tell me he raped you, did you?"

"He didn't. Not...he couldn't get hard. He said it was my fault that...I knew it was because he was insane, but he blamed me. He said...Why are you doing this?"

"Because it's eating you alive knowing that he killed his parents. You're blaming yourself because he raped you and you didn't report it. Not then and not since." Caitlynne nodded at Khan. "He told you his story, now you tell us yours."

"He slammed me against the car and while the limo driver and several other people watched, he ripped my clothes off. All of them until I was naked. Is that what you want to hear? Or is it that he used a bottle on me? Rammed it in my ass so deep I bled for a month. Then when he was through with it, he tried to masturbate over me only to not be able to make himself come that way either." She pulled up her shirt and pointed to the scar there. "So he beat me. Then he pulled out a knife and tried to cut my throat. He tried to kill me."

Khan took her into his arms and glared. Caitlynne smiled. "You think this is funny? You think that making her relive this is some sort of joke?"

"No, but she has to know that we don't care what he did to her before. That we all love her for what she is." Caitlynne walked to Monica and lifted her chin. "It's not your fault that he killed them. You tried to tell them all."

"But I didn't tell them all of it. I should have told them what he'd done to me and maybe he would have gotten help and off the streets."

"No, he wouldn't have. His parents gave him everything he wanted, including you. And for as much as I hate to tell you this right now, he did worse to others like you. We found evidence at his mother's home that she and his father had been paying off families for a decade. He's murdered at least four more women. And it's not your fault." Caitlynne handed her the check she'd given her. "This helped us. More than you can know. This account is the one they used to pay off the families. The only one that the government didn't know about when he took the senate seat and the only one we couldn't monitor. It's why they divorced, so that she could keep it as quiet as they had."

Monica took the check with trembling hands. "He gave me this the morning after I was raped. He said if I kept quiet and cashed it, there would be more. But I had to agree by cashing it."

"Christ." They all turned to look at Reed. "Look what I just found." There were numbers and plenty of them. More than they had first thought, maybe as many as fifteen.

"I don't understand. What are we looking at?" Monica looked at her for an answer. "They're just check amounts with people's names."

Caitlynne waited, knowing that she would understand. And when Monica did, she was glad that Khan was holding her. "No. That's not possible. Please tell me that he didn't kill all those girls."

"I'm sorry. So sorry, but we had to look and you helped us. You made it so we could find them. All of them." Caitlynne looked at Khan. "She never cashed the check the elder Barr gave her and kept it all this time. Without it, without those account numbers, he might have gone on killing. Had she not been as strong or as resilient, he would have kept on going."

"She's my mate. Of course she would be strong." Khan picked her up and sat with her on his lap. "Now that we've all been shocked a little, why don't you tell us what we really want to know? How to kill this bastard."

~~~

Tony tried to call his father again. He wanted answers and he wanted them now. Monica hadn't been around for a couple of days now and he wanted to know where she had friends so he could go and talk to them about her. Next call went to his mother.

"Hello?"

He was startled by the voice, but couldn't quite understand why. Who did he expect to answer the phone but his mother? But the voice wasn't quite right. When the woman on the other end said it again, he smiled and answered her.

"Is my mother there? I've been trying to talk to my dad, but he's not answering either. I want to get him to look something up for me." The person was quiet. "Is she at one of her meetings again? Can you have her call me?" He ended the call and put the phone down. Tony tried to get his mind to let go of something, but he couldn't get it to. Pounding his fists to his forehead, he tried, but there was nothing. Finally, he laid his head down on the bed and closed his eyes.

Nothing was going right. He'd been trying to find his Monica for two days, and still she wasn't around. He'd even gone back to the hotel where he'd seen her, and he wasn't able to get anyone to tell him anything there either. No matter how hard he'd tried. Then at the Mild Pepper, the restaurant he'd thought he'd seen her enter, there was…he tried to think what had happened there and his head felt as if it were zinging.

Tony needed to find her. Monica was going to make sure he didn't have any more headaches. And she'd keep him from having to stay in the hospital.

"No more hospitals. I don't like hospitals." He rolled to his side and stuck his thumb in his mouth. "No more."

The noises in his head were calming now. He could think past the pain, but all the blood was still there. It was bright and it was all over him. When he tried to think where he'd seen all the blood, all he could remember was a fireplace. When things got quiet, he looked at the bruises on his hand.

"There, there now, Tony, you're going to be just fine. Just fine indeed." He laughed at his own voice. "You're going to be just fine."

They always said that. All of them. The girls had said it would be fine, they'd help him with his little problem. He didn't have a problem, it was them. All of it was them. He heard the voices again and tried calming himself. That worked, and he lay there very quietly while he thought calm thoughts. He liked thinking about calm things.

"Trees in the wind. I like trees in the wind. They dance like a kite does. Kites are pretty until they get caught in trees." His head started to beat hard and he went back to calm things. "Kittens are pretty and soft. And ice cream, I very much like ice cream on a hot day."

He kept saying the calming things like they'd told him in the place his mother had put him when he was a child. He'd been there for ages it had seemed, and she'd never come to see him. His father did. And brought him gifts. Tony decided to add gifts to his calm things. He decided that mothers were off the list now and forever.

Tony sat up when his head no longer zinged. He looked around the room, thinking he'd never seen it before and maybe someone had moved him. He tried to remember getting here, and all he could think was someone had moved him while he'd been asleep.

"I don't like to be moved," he yelled to the room. "Do you hear me? I don't like to be moved. I hate it, as a matter of fact."

Standing up, he saw his clothes lying on the floor. When he went to pick them up, he noticed the blood. They were covered in blood. Dropping to his knees, he held his head when it starting pounding. Blood, fireplaces, and cheese. He saw a bell like the kind on a counter, beer in a can. Tony tried to make sense of the things flashing before his eyes, but it was going by much too fast, and he couldn't keep it straight. Looking at the bed again, he crawled to it and climbed into it. No amount of calm thoughts were going to take this away, and he cried out for Monica.

"She'll make them go away. No one will be able to put me away again." He sucked on his thumb again and talked to himself around it. "The others didn't help me like Monica will. You'll see. She'll be the one that will keep me from hurting people. I don't hurt many, but I have to hurt some. Yes, just some."

When he woke, it was dark. He hadn't realized that he had fallen asleep and thought of the nurses that used to come in and make him tired. The ones that had...his head started zinging again. "No, you don't. We aren't going off on that tangent again. No we are not. We have to stay focused and our head on straight. How are we going to appear normal if..."

Tony remembered his father saying that to him one day. They'd been in his father's office and he had just...what had he done? He'd been bad again. Bad with someone. Trying to sort it out, he remembered what they had said to him. The nurses.

"Such a pretty boy, and so big too." He'd been in the bed when they'd said that too him. "A pretty boy who is going to give me what I want."

"They wanted something from me. Everyone wants something from me." He wasn't sure what, but he knew that people had been taking from him. "Taking and taking until I had to make them stop."

Just how he made them stop was not clear. "That's why you have to stay focused, son."

Tony giggled and pulled the blanket up to his chin. His dad would be so proud of him if he could see him now. He was calm and focused. Tony picked up his cell phone again and dialed his father's number. This time instead of ringing, it went to voicemail. He thought his father an important man and ended the call. He would try later.

Closing his eyes again, he relaxed. He was exhausted and sore. His arms hurt, and his hand did as well. When he tried to think how he'd hurt himself, the same pictures flashed in his eyes. Blocking them out as best he could, he worked his toes to uncurl, to relax.

He moved up his body as he'd been told to do when he couldn't sleep. First, his toes. Then, his calves. His knees were next then up his thighs. When he would lose his place, he simply started over. Toes, knees, then thighs, each time moving up his body slowly and making himself be calm. When he was relaxed enough, he let his body go, and he drifted away.

The phone ringing woke him. By the time he realized that it was not the phone but an alarm, he was wide awake. He stretch and then got up. There were clothes on the floor, but he ignored them and went toward the shower. Tony felt great, fantastic even.

"This is going to be the day. I'm going to find my love and we're going to go to my mother's house and plan a big wedding for next month. January will be a new month and a new beginning." He turned on the television as he walked by it.

By the time he was finished in the bathroom, he was starving. Stepping over to the phone to order room service, he caught a glimpse of his father on the television. Reaching for the remote, he wondered what he'd done now and was surprised when the view turned to his mother's house. Turning the volume up, he watched as the police and other people moved around in the yard of his mother's home.

"...sometime yesterday afternoon. The police aren't saying anything right now, but sources tell us that it was brutal and they are both dead."

"Do we know if it was a break-in or not, Shanna? I understand that the Barrs were divorced. Can they tell us why Senator Barr was at the home of his ex-wife?"

"It is my understanding that they had a standing date, as it were, to meet every Wednesday. The senator would come over around two in the afternoon and stay until nine or so, but was always gone by ten. The neighbors around here are shocked by this. They said that both of the Barrs were good, upstanding people."

Tony turned it off. His parents were dead? When? How? Why hadn't anyone gotten in touch with him? And why did he have to learn about it from the news stations instead of before now? He sat on the bed and tried to remember the last time he'd talked to them. His father often, but his mother? He didn't know. He knew that she'd been... Tony needed to contact Monica. The wedding would have to be postponed, of course, and if there were any gifts yet, then they would have to be returned until later.

Tony wasn't sure what to do. He wanted to talk to Monica. Monica had to be... He looked at the remote in his hand and the phone on the bedside table. He had to find her. This was her fault. Had she just...he couldn't remember what, but now he knew that it was completely her fault.

Kathi S. Barton

Chapter Nine

Monica sat in the window seat and watched the ground below her. She had no idea how long she'd been there, but she supposed it was for a while. Khan had come up for a little while, and when she'd asked to be alone, he'd left, but she knew he hadn't wanted to. Then when he'd come to bed, she'd pretended to be asleep until she came to be sitting here. He hadn't moved since.

"You can tell me if you want to."

His voice didn't startle her like she thought it should have.

"What's wrong? Are you still thinking about Barr?"

"Some, but not all." She continued looking out the window. "Caitlynne said that he would be caught, and when he was, she'd make sure he never got out."

"She's someone you can trust. Her word is her bond." Khan didn't get up, but she heard him shift around on the bed. "What else is bothering you?"

What wasn't? she wanted to ask him. But she watched a deer walk through the snow nibbling on grass. She decided that she would ask some of the questions she had about being his mate. "This thing, this mate thing, you said that we're a mated pair. What does that mean? I'll be cat too?" He moved again and she knew he was uncomfortable with the question. Or the answer.

"No. Converting a human to cat is very dangerous. When Walker converted Caitlynne, he said that his cat had done it. He said that—"

"His cat? You mean you have no control over your own body when you're a panther?" She heard the panic, but didn't care. "You mean you can hurt me when you're a cat?"

"No, I didn't mean it that way. I have full control over him even during sex, but sometimes he...he sort of convinces us that things could be this way or that. Like with Caitlynne. Walker's cat wanted her changed, and he convinced Walker that it was a good idea." She didn't like the sound of that and told him so. "It's like when you know something is a bad idea even when you're doing it, but it sounds so good at the time, you let yourself believe that things will work out. That's the way that Walker explained it."

"Did you get those thoughts when we had sex?" She wasn't sure if she really wanted the answer, but now that the question was out there, she thought she did.

"Yes. All the time when I'm with you, even when I'm not with you." She looked over at him when he spoke. His voice had taken on that purr again, and it was low and full of sex.

"Will you? Change me? Will you convert me, Khan?" She thought about what Caitlynne had told her. The bite was painful and hurt, but when she woke up from it, she felt...well, she said she'd felt fucking mother of God fantastic.

"I would love to have you running by my side when I'm in the woods. I want to see you sleek and black, your fur shining under the moonlight. I would love to take you as a cat, lean over you while you're her and take you hard on the ground." Her body responded to his descriptions. "Come here, Monica. Come here and let me show you how I would take you."

She moved as if in a dream. When she stepped away from the window, the moonlight washed over his skin, and she could see every muscle, every defined shape of him, and thought about his cat. Standing still, she took off her shirt and dropped it on the floor. She wanted him, but she wanted him to want her too.

"When you look at me this way, all I can think about is you deep inside of me. I can feel your cock as it touches me in those places that send me over the edge. I love when you suckle at my nipples." She lifted them up and circled her nipples with her fingers. "I love it when you suck them hard and make them tight."

"Come here." His voice held a command, compulsion she'd been told, but she fought it and waited for him to come to her. When he stood up and walked to her, she could see that he was hard, straining from his body. She reached out to touch him when he was close enough.

"So hard and soft. Your cock is as thick as my wrist and all mine." She started to run her hand up and down him, but he wrapped his hand over hers. "I want to taste you like this. I want to take you into my mouth and feel you come there."

He growled at her and she dropped to her knees. Not letting go of him, she licked the thick crown and then took it into her mouth, catching the pearl of cum there on the tip. Moaning, she licked him from root to tip and looked up at him.

"I've never done this before. Tell me how to make you come." His short bark of laughter nearly had her move away from him, but he wrapped his hand in her hair and guided her back to his cock.

"You do any better than you just did and I'm going to die." She licked at him again when he fisted his cock and held it for her. "I want to feel your mouth around me. I want to fuck you this way, pump in and out of your sweet mouth and touch the back of your throat until I come down it."

She did as he asked until he stopped speaking. Monica held onto his hips as she took him in her mouth and bobbed her head over him. Christ, he was delicious, and every time she tasted more of him, she felt her eyes roll in the back of her head. But she wanted more still.

Cupping his balls in her hand, she rolled them around until she thought she could get them into her mouth. Letting go of his cock, she suckled one and rolled it with her tongue. His body became hard, and she felt his hand curl tighter in her hair. When he pulled her away from her feast, she nearly snarled at him. He told her to open, commanded it, and his cock was in her mouth, down her throat, and he was fucking her hard. Swallowing, she felt him slide past the tightness and down. When he came, she gagged slightly, but swallowed again, and he cried out his release.

Her body was screaming for her to do something, anything to ease the ache between her own thighs. As she slid her hand down her body and to her wet pussy, she was being jerked up off the floor and tossed onto the bed.

"My turn." Before she could ask what he meant, he was suckling at her clit. It only took a second for her release to take her, but he didn't stop, not even when she begged him to. When he pressed his fingers, several of them by the feel, deep into her, she rode him as another then another climax took her. When he finally lifted his head, she thought he was finished, she knew that she was, but he only moved up her body, biting and laving her tiny hurt with his tongue.

"I'm going to mount you and then mark you again. Roll over and put your ass up for me to fuck you." She nearly panicked, nearly told him no when he rolled her over and lifted her. "I won't hurt you, not ever, but I need to take you, give my cat a chance to mark you." He entered her hard; her body primed and ready for him, he slid deep. When she raised her head to move back against him, she felt a sting of his hand over her ass.

"I said it's my turn. I take you now and you'll come like this." His hand came down again and she moaned deep. "You like this, don't you? You like me fucking you and spanking you."

His hand came down twice more, and she came both times. When he leaned over her and pinched her clit, she came apart, screaming out his name and begging him to come. When he licked along her shoulder, she bared her throat for him, and when he bit, she screamed again through one of the hardest climaxes she'd ever had.

Monica dimly heard him shout out his own release, felt him collapse over her. His weight dead against her own, she tried to hold them both up. When she dropped on the bed, he rolled over to his back, taking her with him.

"I love you, Monica. I love you more than I've ever dreamed possible."

She felt a blanket cover them, and she snuggled under his arm when she rolled over. She yawned and wrapped her hand into his chest hair. "I love you too." She closed her eyes and felt herself drifting off the sleep. His snores, loud and near her ear, didn't bother her as much as she thought they might, and she fell asleep with a smile on her face.

~~~

Khan reached for her and felt a cold sheet. Rolling over to see if he missed her, he saw that she was gone. Smiling, he remembered the four or five times he'd reached for her last night, and she'd responded to him willingly each time.

He got up and went to the shower to get cleaned up and go find her. He wanted to tell her that he wanted to wake with her beside him from now on. He stopped brushing his teeth for a second and reworded it in his mind. He'd *prefer* that she was there when he woke, so he could make love to her first thing in the morning. Smiling, he took a quick shower and dressed.

She was standing over the stove, cooking something. He looked over at Sebastian and raised his brow when his brother shook his head. Something was going on and it didn't seem like it was a good thing. He walked up behind her and looked over her shoulder at...he wasn't sure what.

"Want some help?" She turned slightly, and he could see that her eyes were filled with unshed tears. He nearly took the pan from her when Reed spoke up from behind him.

"She said she knew how to cook at one time, but it's been awhile. We told her we'd be her lab rats." Reed was trying to sound cheerful, but he sounded like he was upset too.

"I was a really good cook a long time ago. And I could make a really good omelet. I think I've forgotten how." She looked ready to toss the pan in the sink. He wanted to tell her to go sit down, he'd take care of it, but he only got more eggs out of refrigerator.

"I like western omelets myself." He looked at his brothers. "Reed, why don't you chop up the peppers, and Sebastian, can you make some potatoes? How do Obrien's sound?"

He moved around her, took the pan with the mess in it, and handed her a fresh one. He said something about the incorrect cooking pans, and why were there so many, when she sprayed it with the oil. Handing her the bowl of beaten eggs, he watched her pour them in the pan and stir them around the edges so they could cook quicker. She seemed to be getting the hang of it when he turned to Sebastian.

He'd cut up some of the leftover baked potatoes they'd had last night for dinner and had some onions on the same cutting board. Sliding them in another pan, he tossed them around until they were hot and browned. Keeping an eye on Monica, who was making the second pan full of eggs, he asked for and received four plates.

By the time they were ready to eat, she was making jokes about confidence, and his brothers were laughing with her. He was just glad they'd kept their mouths shut about the mess she'd first made.

"How is your link working? Have you figured out how to speak to all of us yet?" Sebastian looked at Khan when he spoke. "I still have trouble with Caitlynne at times; she tends to block when she's stressed."

"What link thing?" She took another bite of eggs and looked at him. "I would think that Caitlynne was good with computers."

He laughed and reached to her mind. *"He means speaking like this. We have our own line of private communication, and we'll have one with all of them, my family, as well."*

He watched her face when she didn't respond back to him. When she put down her fork and looked at Sebastian, he burst out laughing.

"She got me. Reed?"

He nodded too, grinning at her like she was a prize he'd just won at the fair. When she turned to Khan, he watched her face and knew she was trying. He connected with her again. *"Follow it back to me. You should be able to send me thoughts anytime you want."* He was nearly ready to tell her not to try so hard when he was flooded with warmth and love. *"That's it, baby. Perfect. Can you speak to me?"*

"I don't know, it makes my head hurt. I can…I can speak to Walker too. He's with the president and Marshall. He said to tell you he wants omelets tomorrow." She grinned at him.

"Tell Walker he can make his own—" She cut him off verbally and for now he was fine with that. He was more concerned with her speaking to Walker.

"Not Walker, the president. He wants the omelets. Walker said he has his wife cook for him."

Khan didn't move. *"You mean Walker told you the president wanted omelets. You mean he relayed the information to you."* She shook her head. *"Monica, honey, you can't talk to other species. Only panthers."*

"I don't know what you mean. I'm talking to the president, and his aide, Marshall, said that you should believe him. Warren said he's going to call you right now."

Khan's phone rang and he nearly had a heart attack. When he answered, he was surprised by the laughter.

"She most certainly talked to me, both of us. How the hell is she able to do that?" Khan told him he didn't know. "Well I got to tell you, it'll be damned helpful to me if I could borrow her for special occasions. Could help me work out a great many deals with others, if you know what I mean."

Khan nodded. "I guess it would. I had no idea that anyone could do that." Khan took her hand and realized how cold it was. He kissed it and smiled at her, but in truth, he was afraid for her. People would kill her for what she could do.

After ending the call with Warren, they all cleaned up the kitchen. Monica was quiet, but the boys more than made up for the lack of responses from her. He knew they had heard what had happened, but they'd not said anything. When they left the kitchen, thanking her for cooking for them, she sat down.

"Am I in trouble? Because if I am, I want to know right now." She pounded her fists on the table. "Right now, Khan."

"Why on earth would you be in trouble? I mean, I'm afraid for you. If someone, another species, finds out you can listen in on the conversations that are for their packs or groups, they may get a tad pissy, but you're not in trouble."

"Then tell me why I can do this. I want to know why you looked so…ashamed of me because I could talk to Warren."

"Ashamed? Of you? Never. Christ, what I wouldn't give to know what someone I'm talking to is thinking. If they are planning an attack or if they have five hundred of their kind on my porch. But ashamed? No, I love you." He kneeled down in front of her. "You are so wonderful and special to me that I can't help but be mesmerized by you every time I look at you."

She laughed. "Okay, that was a little over the top. Good, but too much."

He kissed her. "I'm working on it. Bear with me, okay?"

Kathi S. Barton

Chapter Ten

Dylan sat in the kitchen. He'd been traveling all day and he was tired. He had to drive back tonight too, as he had class in the morning. But when Reed had called him, he knew it was important to Khan and Monica that he make the trip. When the pretty little maid told him that Mr. Khan and Miss Monica were on their way, she winked at him. Dylan, never one to pass up a chance to get laid, winked back.

When they both walked in, he stood up. The girl had certainly changed from the last time he'd seen her. He nodded to her, then shook her hand and hugged Khan. They had their differences and plenty of them, but they were brothers first and foremost.

"I thought you couldn't get away." Dylan nodded at Khan's statement. "But you drove all the way up here when you could have flown with us."

"So I did. I have to talk to you both. It's important." When the maid left the room, Dylan leaned in his chair to watch her walk away. He sure loved a woman's ass. When Khan cleared his throat and Monica giggled, he sat up.

"What couldn't be done over the phone, Dylan? It's four in the morning. And I don't know if you've heard or not, but someone is trying to kill my mate."

Dylan had heard, but that wasn't why he was here. "Reed called me last night. I wanted to talk to you about a couple of things." He reached into his bag and pulled out a scroll. "It's very old, so be careful with it. Mom doesn't know I have it."

"Good thing too. She'd kill you. What the hell are you doing with the family tree? And the original one at that." Khan touched it gently. Dylan didn't blame him. It was as old as their race was.

"I needed to show you something. Mostly Monica, but I wanted you to see this." He pointed to the name of a person that had been born and had died long before their grandmother had. "Her name is Elizza Manchester Bowen. She was our great-great-grandmother."

Each of them looked at the name, but Monica noticed what he was trying to get them to see. She leaned into the parchment and squinted before she was able to read it aloud. When she did, she looked at him. "It says 'no boundaries.' What does that mean?"

He felt her touch his mind and he let her. This was the only way she'd learn.

"It means she could hear all the other species like you can." She leaned back in the chair so quickly she nearly tipped it over. "You're not the only panther to have this ability."

"How do you know this? She's been dead so long, for all you know it could mean she wouldn't stay on her own land and didn't know any boundaries." Khan stood up to pace, and Dylan watched Monica. "This is the most... Is that why you came up here in the middle of the night? To give us your opinion on old folk tales?"

"He's telling the truth. They're not tales. She really could do what I can." She looked him in the eye. "What you can as well."

Dylan nodded and didn't look at his brother. "Since childhood. I was terrified when I figured out that none of the rest of them could do it, but when I saw this...I asked my grandda and he told me what it meant and what happened to her."

Khan sat down hard. "You're like Monica? You can hear other species as well? How is that possible?"

Dylan laughed. "It's as much a part of you as it is me. Had it not been, then she wouldn't be like us either. And she is. We can hear things, know things that others can't."

"Why didn't I know about this? Why didn't...why did Reed know about this?"

Dylan heard the hurt in Khan's voice. "He didn't. He was relaying the events of the day as he's done since you got here. He doesn't..." Dylan got up, got a bottle of water from the refrigerator, and sat back down. He knew that neither of them wanted any.

"None of you know." Monica looked at Khan. "He didn't want any of you to know because he was ashamed at first then later he felt it was too late."

"You two want me to leave the room?" Khan got up to pace again. "I don't want you talking to her like that. You know that we're newly mated and—"

"She was reading my mind. I didn't say a word to her that you've not heard. She's a lot better at this than I was when I figured it out." Dylan grinned at her. "Tell him, sweetheart, before he tries to rip my throat out."

"I wasn't trying to cause trouble. I was...it seemed the thing to do. I didn't even know I could do that." She put her hands on her lap. "You could have told me to stop."

"Yeah, but what fun would that be?" Dylan got up and pulled things from the refrigerator. "I want to stay today, but then I have to go back tonight. I have exams to grade and a few guys I have to beat at poker tomorrow night. I need to win back some of the gas money it took me to get here." He didn't need the money any more than the rest of them did. Caitlynne had seen to that. She'd paid off all their outstanding loans and had given each of them a nice tidy nest egg as well. He hadn't touched his and probably never would, but it was nice to have there just in case. As he fried up bacon, he spoke to them both. "I can teach you as much as I can today, if you don't mind. I figure with this guy whose trying to kill you, it would be nice to have a little extra on your side." He turned to her as she pulled out the plates.

"That won't help us much, I'm afraid. The man who is after me is human. I guess he's like me."

Dylan stopped putting more bacon in the pan and looked at her.

"You knew that, didn't you? I'm sorry you wasted your gas money, but—"

"Monica, he's a species just like us. Human is a species, and you're nothing close to being human any longer. You might not be able to shift, but you aren't human any longer." Dylan looked at his brother. "Tell her. Tell her she's not human."

"What is she then if not that? I don't understand what you mean." Khan sounded pissy again, and he looked between them. Dylan nearly burst out laughing, but Khan was holding a large skillet.

"She's as much a panther as you. You didn't convert her yet, but she has enough panther blood in her system that if she were to carry, the baby would be full-blooded." Monica looked at Khan. "I'm not lying to you, bro. She's as near panther as you can get without the entire shift fun."

Monica changed the subject, but not before she whispered in his mind. *"Do behave, will you? This is hard enough on both of us."* "What do you mean Tony is a species? I understand the concept of him being a species, but I thought that I could only hear paranormals."

"No. You know no boundaries." He asked them to wait a moment, and he left the room to get the pretty maid. He made sure he touched her skin. When they entered the kitchen, Dylan introduced them to her. "This is Molly. Molly works here not because she likes the work, but she steals food from the pantry each night to take home to her family. What she doesn't know is that everyone in the house that works here knows and replaces it for her. They don't want her to lose her job." He got that bit of information from the man who had let him in this morning, but he hadn't known who Molly was.

Molly sat down and looked around the room. "Don't tell Miss Caitlynne. She'll fire me for sure."

"We won't, but you have to help us with something." He looked at Monica. "Read her mind." He could tell she was trying, but from the look on her face, she got nothing. Dylan told her to touch her skin. "But not her hands. I don't know why, but for some reason, that doesn't work."

Monica touched her arm and then stepped back. "Her husband left her about nine months ago for another woman. Molly is not just struggling to make ends meet, but she's also trying her best to get her little sister into med school so she doesn't have to wait tables for the rest of her life."

Molly nodded, but didn't move. "He took everything when he left us for her. Everything including the microwave. Jane and I have been trying to make it stick for us, but school is expensive, and her books cost more than a car. I don't...you won't tell Miss Caitlynne, will you? You promised if I helped you, I wouldn't get fired."

"And you won't either." Both Dylan and Khan reached for their wallets at the same time and were just about to pull them out when Monica continued. "Caitlynne has a fund set up for people who want to better themselves. I bet if you had a talk with her, you and your sister, she can help you in ways you wouldn't believe. Of course you'll have to come clean about the food, but I bet you she won't mind a wit and will tell you to take more."

Dylan looked over at Khan, who looked like he'd just won the lottery. "My mate. She's going to be amazing at family dinners."

Dylan thought he might be right. After sending Molly to find the mistress of the house, Dylan worked with Monica a little more. She was going to be fine once he had more time and she wasn't so stressed about Tony. And Dylan knew that if they didn't find him, he would, and kill him slowly.

When Monica left to get dressed, Dylan looked at Khan. "He hurt her. He hurt her more than she's shared with any of you. He shouldn't be allowed to breathe."

Khan looked at him with both surprise and wonderment. Before he could ask him what he meant, Dylan raised his hand. He wouldn't share that information unless she let him or it was to save her life.

"I'll take care of him. With what she has shared, it's enough to bring all of us on his ass. If I find him before the police do ,and I plan on that happening...he's going to suffer in ways you can't believe."

~~~

Monica's mind hurt along with her head. Dylan had left just under an hour ago and she was still reeling from all he'd told her. Most of which had to do with reading others' minds.

It wasn't really hard. She only had to concentrate a little and so much information came to her. Dylan had told her it was because most people didn't know there were people like them and didn't try to hide what they thought. But the two of them knew and they had to be careful, very careful.

"And you must at all costs learn to block people. Because if you can get in, they can as well. Don't trust anyone to your mind. There is way too much in there for others to know."

"You mean about you being panthers."

He nodded at her and smiled.

"Do you think there are others like you?"

"You mean panthers or like you and me? And for the record, you're a panther too. Like I said, as close as you can get." He had leaned back and smiled at her. "You know that there are. And if one comes in the room with you, at least within a twenty to twenty-five foot radius, you'll know they're there too."

She worked on blocking her mind all day and now needed a nap. And she decided that she didn't want to take it alone. Almost getting up off the couch, she closed her eyes and tried to find Khan in the house. He was in the office with his brother, Walker. She decided to try something.

She didn't know what sort of images she could use in the event that someone else could see them. Dylan had told her that they couldn't, but she wasn't quite that sure yet. She decided to try them out, but to go kind of slow at it.

At first she sent him the thought of just her naked and in the shower. She wanted to bring him running, not bore him, and she made her hands slide down her body. She lifted her breasts up and licked the tip of each one. Moaning a little, she moved her hands down her body and slid her fingers into her pussy and moaned aloud when she brushed against her clit. Over and over she slid past her silken folds until she was panting. She lifted her breast again and nipped gently at the tip and then suckled it in her mouth. She didn't know if it was possible to do that, but she decided to try next time she was in the shower. When the door slammed back against the wall, she looked at Khan. She'd forgotten that she was teasing him.

"Strip."

Her body reacted to his command.

"Now. I want you to do to what you showed me. Now, Monica, I want to see it now."

His cock was hard against the fabric of his jeans, and she licked her lips. She wanted him to touch her, to do the things she'd been doing, but he shook his head and told her again to show him.

She stood up, thinking to go to the bedroom and show him when he unsnapped his jeans and freed his cock. She looked at him while he fisted himself, using his precum to slide up and down his shaft.

"You want this?"

She nodded.

"Then you'll do as I ask. Do you have any idea what you did to me in there? Do you have a clue what happened to me when I saw you take your nipple into your mouth and fuck your pussy?"

"I wanted to make you come to me."

He laughed, but it was strained.

"I guess I did that, didn't I?"

"Yes. Show me, Monica. Show me for real what you want to do to yourself."

She wanted to please him, and she wanted him to want her. Stripping down wasn't as hard as she thought it would be. They'd had sex in every part of this house, and some places in the yard, enough that he had made her feel good about herself and her body. When she was naked, she stopped.

"Your turn. I want to have you there so I can think about you touching me, you sliding in and out of me as I touch myself. You have to help me."

His clothes came off quicker than hers had. When he stood there in all his beauty, she looked him up and down, lingering over the parts of him that she so desperately wanted.

Cupping her breast, she held it to her mouth. Licking her lips as he watched her, she flicked her tongue over the hard nubbin. She moaned; it was much better than she thought it would feel. Doing it again, she watched as he wrapped his fist around his cock and moved up and down it slowly, his balls tight against his body.

When she pulled her nipple into her mouth, she felt her pussy clench. Her juices were flowing down her legs, and she parted them so that he could see. She slid her hand down over her belly, twirled her finger into her belly button, and bit down on her nipple.

"Christ. You're going to make me come this way. I'm going to shoot my cum all over your body then I'm going to take you to the floor and fuck you hard."

Bolder now, she moved to her pussy and put two of her fingers deep. Using her other hand, she opened her nether lips so she could touch herself better and to let Khan see her. She had no idea what she was doing, but it felt so good she didn't stop. Suddenly, her hands were brushed aside and Khan was taking her into his mouth.

She came the moment he bit down on her clit. Screaming out his name, she curled her hand into his hair and held him to her as she rode his mouth. Each time he nipped at her, bringing her close, he would slow until she was calm. She decided the next time she played with him, she was going to do it from very far away.

"I have to be inside of you. Now." He lay on his back and pulled her down. "Ride me. Ride me like you were your fingers. I want to feel you come on me this way."

She lowered herself over his cock slowly. She knew that he wanted her to hurry, but he didn't push her. When she was seated over him as far as she could go, he grabbed her hips and showed her how to ride. When she leaned forward, using his chest as a brace, he reached up and squeezed her nipples until she thought she was going to die from the pain/pleasure of it. When she came this time she had no buildup; Khan had jerked her over the edge by leaning up and biting her breast hard. Even as he suckled from her, she felt his cock shoot his cum deep. When he rolled her to her back, he lifted her legs to his shoulder and leaned into her.

"Cum again. I want you to cum with me inside you this deep."

Her body did as he commanded and she saw stars burst behind her eyelids. When he came this time, he cried out her name and said that he loved her.

Khan lifted his weight off her and let her legs fall to the floor. She couldn't move, and apparently he couldn't very well either. After he reached up and pulled the afghan off the back of the couch, he covered them both and pulled her into his arms. She heard his snores seconds later. Resting her head on his chest, she closed her eyes too and wondered what the household would think when they found them there.

Chapter Eleven

Tony watched the news again and again. Each time, he was not mentioned. He held his cell phone in his hand in the event that the ringer was broken, waiting for someone to call him and let him know what was going on.

His parents were dead.

He wanted to go back home, to see for himself that they were really dead, but something held him back. Flashes of fireplaces and cheese kept him away. He had looked at the bloodied shirt and wondered if someone had tried to kill him as well and he'd gotten away. Then the story of the hotel manager came on.

He didn't know why that place gave him head pains. The front of it was marked off in yellow police tape as well. But, again, something kept him from there. It was the place where he'd talked to Monica, but there was something else. Something that he didn't want to remember.

When a commercial came on, he moved to the bed and curled in his ball. He stuck his thumb in his mouth and lay there, curling his fingers in his hair. It didn't calm him as much as it had before. Something…Monica was keeping him from resting.

She hadn't helped him like he'd thought she would. She'd been like the others. They only wanted to take and take until there was nothing left for him. And Tony had decided it was time to take himself back. Rolling to his back, he continued to suck his thumb. She would have to be dealt with.

Like the others, she needed to be punished. Not to be gone, but like the others, she needed to learn that he wasn't to be played with. He needed her and she'd failed him. Tony looked at the television again when another news story came on. This one was about an accident, but it didn't hold his attention or upset him like the other stories had. This one he could watch.

"Where are you?" He looked around the room, wanting someone to answer him. "I've been good. I want you all to just leave me alone."

He lay back down and stuck his thumb in his mouth. They never would and he knew it. Tony started on his calm words and only got to three before he got up and went to the television. Screaming at it hadn't helped earlier, and turning it off hadn't as well. Someone had come in and turned it right back on again. Tony couldn't win.

Reaching under the mattress, he pulled out the gun. He'd found it in his mother's house, and he...he couldn't remember when he'd found it, but now it was his. All of her stuff and his father's was now his. Rubbing the barrel over his cheek, he thought that it was something he could do forever. The smooth, cool metal over his cheek made him happy. Happy in ways that he'd not been since... He shut out the thought of happiness and thought of the gun and the way it made him feel.

But he had it for a reason and he was ready to find her and use it. Glancing at the television, he froze. He knew her. That woman he knew. Crawling on his hands and knees to get closer, he watched her speak in the microphone. She was talking about his father and his mother.

"They were well liked, and the community will feel the loss of them for many, many years to come. Senator Barr had served several terms on the seat until his retirement earlier this year. He will, like his wife, be sorely missed." She turned to someone to her left and nodded.

"Do you have any leads on the killer? Anything you can tell the press?"

The camera panned to a little man with a hat on. Then back to the woman before she spoke.

"We are pursuing a lead now and have gotten all the men working overtime to find their killer. And we will bring this person to justice. I can tell you that the murders were brutal and the act of one person. No one else was at home when the murders occurred." She pulled up a picture and showed it to the camera. "If anyone has any information on this vehicle, please contact my office. We are only asking to speak to this individual; that is all at this time."

Tony got up and looked out the window to his hotel room. He was much too far up to see down to the parking garage, but he was pretty sure his car had been stolen. That lady, Caitlynne Bowen, had shown his car on television and had not told anyone who he was.

He was standing at the door when he glanced at the television again. He nearly fell over getting back to it. There she was, his Monica. He watched her as two men stood next to her. Two men he didn't…peering closer, he *did* know one of them. Tony beat on his head trying to remember where. He had a feeling it was important, but the more he beat on his head, the more he couldn't remember. Going to the bed, he crawled into it and curled up.

"Remember, remember, remember. Calm thoughts, Tony, calm thoughts. Rain, sunshine, flowers, cats, dogs. Calm, Tony, calming thoughts. He was on his fourth list of calm words he'd been using for the past two days when he remembered. "Ah ha. You were in her room when I went there to speak to her." He looked at the television and they were all gone. The news was over and his Monica was gone. He knew that he'd not be able to rewind it or to make it come back, but he knew where she was now. His Monica was with that woman Bowen.

This time when he went to the door, he had packed up all this things. He decided to leave his bloodied shirt behind. He wasn't even sure now that it was his. And since he wasn't sure, he wasn't going to soil his clothes with that one.

His car was still there. Tony couldn't really believe now that he'd thought the one that the Bowen woman was showing everyone was his. He hadn't left the hotel for...the pain in his head made him stop thinking about it, and he got in his car. Smiling, he drove out of the garage and onto the street.

Getting to the house proved to be difficult. He couldn't remember names of streets, and the house number and street name kept skittering away when he tried to recall it. He thought about stopping and asking for directions, but that, too, hurt him. He finally had to pull over and crawl into the back seat to close his eyes. As soon as he closed his eyes, he drifted away.

He'd been five when they'd put him away the first time. He'd done something bad, really bad. But his mind wouldn't, or couldn't, he didn't know which, let him see it. There was a crib and a little pink dolly. But he'd spent a long time there and it wasn't too bad. It was when he'd been a teenager that he'd really been afraid.

He didn't know why he'd woken up there. He'd been in his bed the last time he could remember anything and had been jarred awake in That Place. That Place is how he thought of it when he did. And when he did, he always had bad dreams. Horrible, screaming dreams that made him hurt for days.

They had tied him down at first, and no amount of begging would get them to call his father. He'd begged so much that they'd finally put a gag in his mouth. And shutting him up wasn't the only thing they'd used that nasty thing for.

When he'd been there a few days, a nurse came to him and told him it was time for his treatments. He had no idea what that meant. His mother had treatments too, but it usually meant her hair or her body needed to be changed. This treatment wasn't a treat at all.

Tony shifted on the seat and moaned. He knew he was sleeping, but he could also hear things going on around him. He drifted back to the dream when he realized it was nothing more than a horn beeping somewhere close.

They had tied him to a metal bed. He knew it was metal because it had been cold and hard. When they tightened the gag—a ball on a leather strap—into his mouth, he had screamed around it. But no one would listen to him. When the doctor came in and—

He came awake screaming. He hurt now as he had then. A thirteen-year-old boy should not have to do that, he thought, and held his head in his hands. The blood that poured from his nose and ears made him afraid, but he didn't leave the back seat. He knew that if he did, they'd take him back there. He had to find his Monica and make her pay.

This was all Monica's fault.

~~~

Monica sat in the living room and stared at the two men with her. At least one person was with her all the time and when there was no one in the house, as there wasn't now, there were two. And she was pissed about it.

"It's to keep you safe," Khan had told her when she went to him last night. "You can't expect me to like the fact that we're using you as bait to catch a madman. I agreed to this on the condition that you had a bodyguard. And you'll abide by this for me."

She didn't like it, but knew that he wasn't going to relent. She eyed the younger man and decided to practice on him. He seemed to be nice, but she was bored and pissed.

Reaching out to his mind, she made him scratch his head. When he did it, she was delighted. Off and on for an hour she played with him. Nothing dangerous, but just enough fun to keep her from storming over to him and punching him in the nose.

"What is he doing?"

The voice startled her and she looked over at George.

"Is he really dancing with a mop?"

He looked at her and winked. She flushed, pulled out of the younger man's mind, and put him back to rights. She was glad that George didn't ask about the lampshade on his head when the man put it back.

"Having a little fun, are you? I had a long talk with Dylan and he told me about his visit. Thank you for that." George sat down beside her. "You want some real company?"

"Yes, and what are you thanking me for? He helped *me*, not the other way around." She liked the elder Bowen, both of them, as a matter of fact. "What are you doing here? I thought you and Mrs. Bowen were told to stay home."

"We were. But like you, we got bored. And we wanted to see that new show at the theater. I so love going to plays and operas in this town." He patted her on the knee. "I'm thanking you for not freaking out when Dylan had his talk with you and for giving him the push to tell us. It was quite a shock, but we're so happy for him. Both of you, really. Are you..."

He looked over at the young man again. "Ah, practicing, were you? Good. It might be helpful if you have that."

"Khan is mad because they decided the best way to bring this man to justice is to use me as bait. He thinks I only agreed to this to make him pissy. I didn't. He has enough about me that makes him pissy without me trying to add to it." She looked over at George when he laughed. She smiled with him.

"He is a mite protective, is he? Gets that from me. I used to drive my Corrine to madness when we were first mated. Wouldn't let her out of my sight for any reason. Near drove the people she worked with batty too." He grinned huge. "She had me arrested."

"I most certainly did not. Hello, dear. How are you fairing with this old fool?" Corrine kissed her on the cheek and sat across from them. "You really should learn to tell the story correctly if you want to remember the details every time. I had him pulled into the station to have him talked to. The young officer at the time is now the chief of police in our town. Terrance is a good man."

George nodded. "Yes, he is, but a pain in my ass too. You should have heard the things he said to me. Told me that stalking is a crime and that I would end up on the wrong end of a gun if I didn't cease and desist. Damned man even had the nerve to tell me that marrying the girl wouldn't change the facts, but it might make her a tad bit easier on me."

"You married her to keep out of jail?" Monica burst out laughing. "You did not. You love her very much and it shows in everything you do for her. Mr. Bowen, I've never met a more romantic man in my life."

"Now that's just sad." He looked at his wife. "You didn't train them boys to be romantic? I thought that was your job."

"No, Khan is romantic. He bought me flowers once." She tried to remember why and realized it was because he'd made her mad. "I think it was nice. Then he showed me that he was a panther."

"Not romantic if it's to make up for screwing up." George looked ready to go hunt his son down. "I guess I'll have to take him to the woodshed again. Never too old for that, I'm thinking."

"No," she screamed at him. "Don't do that. I don't want any more issues between families because of me. He and Caitlynne aren't seeing eye-to-eye right now because of this thing, and I don't want you two at it either."

She knew as soon as he said he'd leave it alone for now that he'd say something to Khan. She wished that she'd never said anything. But Corrine spoke up, and she tried not to think of it anymore right now.

"Dylan was telling us that you're very strong at the no boundaries...I'm not sure what to call it. Power?" She smiled at Monica. "I'm so glad he told us. I've always had a feeling that he knew more than he should. His great-great grandmother would have that same faraway look in her eyes at times."

"I didn't realize that you knew her. Dylan thought she'd been dead before you were born." Monica looked at George when he laughed.

"If only she had been. The old buzzard knew a great deal all right. Right down to the first time that...well, she knew a lot." George blushed as he continued. "And she had no trouble telling me that my children were going to make me pay for all my misdeeds too. She was right, now that I think on it."

"She was his great grandmother and she loved him dearly." Corrine glared at George and then blew him a kiss as she continued. "But she was a little outspoken. But as young people, we didn't know much about what she was able to do. It's only been as recently as last evening that I found some writings on her. She had kept the books of the Bowen family, you see, and had put a great deal of information in it to make sure that when—and she did say when—another like her showed up, we'd be able to welcome them and not have them put away."

"They put her away?" Corrine nodded at her question. "Then they didn't really trust that she was telling the truth. That's sad."

"It is, but maybe not." Corrine went on to explain. "She was able to learn to control it, which is good. She said in her writings that she thought that it could be transferred from one panther to another through biting, but she wasn't sure. She had four children, all boys, and had been glad that none of them seemed to be cursed with it. She predicted that it would surface again, and she hoped that it would be something more tolerated than it had been when she was around. I think we have come a long way, don't you, dear?"

Monica nodded. She did. She wanted to ask them something else about her and Khan, but one of the household servants came in and said that lunch was ready. He also informed them that Mr. Khan and Mr. Walker would be joining them and that Miss Caitlynne was on a mission.

"A mission. How exciting for her." Corrine took her arm as they moved to the dining room. "Can you imagine all the things she's seen and done?"

Monica nodded. She had. Accidentally, yesterday morning, as a matter of fact, when she'd been playing around. Caitlynne had been asleep and Monica wondered if she could figure out the sex of the baby. It was a boy, but she'd gotten so much more. Things she promised herself she'd never think of again.

Lunch was loud and friendly. Monica sat by George, and he laughed when Khan growled at him. He was man she could easily love, and did. When George reached over and kissed her cheek again, Khan stood up.

"Old man, I don't care if you are my dad, stop flirting with my mate." He sat down again, but didn't stop glaring. "How do you expect to live to see a grandchild if you're constantly pushing the envelope?"

"I will because you love me." He patted her on the shoulder. "You want me to stop, then do right by the girl and wed her. Walker did. It makes a woman know that she's permanent when you put a ring on her finger, don't it, Caitie, my dear?"

Caitlynne walked in and smiled at George before she smacked him on the head. "I told you several times already to stop calling me that stupid name. It's McCray or Caitlynne. Not that insipid name that sounds like I should be drinking milk out of a bowl. And for the record, I will never do that. Hello, everyone. I'm home."

Walker kissed her on the mouth hard and quick. Monica had no doubt that the big man was going to take his wife upstairs and mark her again very soon. Caitlynne had told her yesterday that it was their way of dealing with her being around so many men all the time. She kept her job and no one was killed. Then she smiled. Monica never wondered if she was kidding or not. The woman had a very scary smile.

Chapter Twelve

Khan watched Monica. He could tell she was still mad at him, and he didn't really blame her. He'd been demanding and hard on her about this. He wasn't going to relent on his demands of the bodyguards, but he could see why it made her mad. She liked her privacy.

But when they'd come to him the day before yesterday about the plan, he'd been against it. Against it so harshly that he'd threatened to take her somewhere that they'd never find her and where this Barr person would never find her. Then Marshall spoke up.

"So you're willing to run the rest of your life?"

He looked up at the weretiger.

"You willing to pack your family up, the one you might have with her, and move every few years? Because that's what will happen if this man isn't caught."

"He's one man. I can handle him. If he gets to be too much of an issue, then I'll simply do what is best for my family." Marshall shook his head. "No one will miss him. He's a murderer."

"And so will you be."

That made him shut up and look at Monica as she continued.

"You'll be no different than he is. Killing because you can or because it gets too inconvenient for you? How on earth do you expect me to live with myself if you kill him because of me? How, if we do have children, will they feel knowing that their dad killed a man?"

He opened his mouth to deny what she was saying and that if their children found out, she would have told them, but she cut him off.

"What if they're like me and know?"

So here he was with a houseful of strangers in a house that wasn't his with a mate that was pissed at him. He had to do something. Soon, too, because he didn't like the tension between them. Especially since she wasn't touching him. He wasn't touching her either, but she'd pissed him off. He glanced at Walker and Caitlynne and wanted what they had. His mother kicked him under the table.

"Khan, there's something in the kitchen I need your help with. Do you think you could help me? I've gone overboard buying things for the new baby. I wish for a girl, but will be so happy with a little grandson to bounce on my knee." He followed her into the kitchen and was nearly ready to ask her why she didn't just have one of the millions of people working there do it. But she slapped him hard on the face first.

"What the hell was that for?" When she pointed to a chair, he sat. "Would you mind telling me why I'm on your shit list before I get told to stand in the corner too?" He flushed when she started taping her foot. Not a good sign. Neither was the arms crossed over her chest. Khan tried to think what he'd done and was coming up empty on things she might have heard.

"Are you going to sit there and tell me you don't know?"

He didn't move. It was a trap and he knew it.

"Are you going to marry her or not? Or are you going to simply let being your mate, the almightily Khan Bowen's mate, be enough for her."

He didn't like the way she was painting a picture of him, but wisely kept his mouth shut. "That girl is depressed beyond words. Did you know that she can't contact you? Have you done anything at all about fixing that?"

He looked up at her sharply. "I've made sure she can contact me and I tell her where I'm going every time I leave the house or go to another part of it. She knows where I am better than I do sometimes."

"Can she link with you?"

He looked at the dining room door and back at his mother when she whispered through his mind.

"She spoke to Dylan when he was here. And when he asked her to contact you, she said that you were not there. What if something happens and she needs you where a phone won't work? Being in another part of the house doesn't mean crap if there is someone trying to hurt her where she is."

"She can do it. I…" He tried to think if he'd ever talked to her through their link and knew that they had. Or had they? She'd sent him images of herself, but spoken? He tried to think. "She didn't tell me. She should have told me."

When he stood back up, his mom pushed him back down. "I'm not through with you yet. Do you love her?"

"Yes," he answered without hesitation. "Very much so. I think I have for all of my life. Why? Did she tell you she doesn't love me?"

"No, she didn't. In fact, she's barely mentioned you since we got here. Have you pissed her off?" He nodded. "Then what have you done to make it up to her? Nothing, I would imagine. Did you know that your father asked her about flowers? And she said that you'd bought her some. Was it because you were mad at her and bought them as a peace offering?"

"I wanted to get her something because I'd made her run here. She wouldn't have... What does this have to do with me loving her?" He realized he'd snapped when she stared at him with that "you did not just do that to me" look. "I love her very much, but I'm frightened for her. I want to take her home and keep her there and make her happy."

His mom kissed him on the head and stood up. "Geography doesn't matter when you love someone. You can love her here as well as you could at home. You can show her that you love her just as well here as at home. In fact, there are more ways for you to show her here than there. That's why your father and I are here. He's taking me to the theater because I enjoy it and we can see our stubborn children."

"And he didn't piss you off?"

She laughed at his question and went to the pantry. She handed him a large box and three of the five bags on the floor. "Of course he did, but he doesn't sleep on the floor because of it. He finds a way to make me smile at him." She led the way to the dining room again. "You have a baby soon, and I'll buy you too much as well."

Khan wanted to romance his mate. He just didn't have a clue how. He tried to think if any of his brothers were romantic and decided to call Dylan. He was by far dating the most of all of them and had been from the time he'd discovered girls were fun. But he looked over at Marshall and though the man was gay; he would bet his last dollar that he knew something about romance.

He asked to speak to him after lunch. He'd hinted that it was about the plan, but as soon as the door was closed, he realized how little he even knew about Monica and sat down hard in the chair. He looked up when Marshall laughed.

"It can't be that bad, can it?" Khan nodded and he laughed harder. "Maybe if we plan this out together, we can get you over this. It's the best plan of action for this man. He's murdered so many and—"

"No, that's not it." He got up to pace. "I'm in love with Monica. And I don't know how to romance her. She needs some romance, I think…actually, my whole family thinks she could probably do better than me, but she has me. But I don't have a clue how to go about showing her."

Marshall sat down. "And you came to me because? Never mind. Don't answer that. You want to romance her, then tell her. She's going to be your best information on how to do that. That is unless she's pissed at you."

"She is. A great deal. Before her…well, you knew me before her. I don't know anything about her. Her birthday, her favorite color, nothing."

Marshall reached onto the desk and then handed him a small notebook. "You have to start keeping track of things first of all. Like when you bought her flowers and why. Were you mad at her, or she at you? Did you buy her something you liked, or that she liked? This may sound silly, but it will help you. And her birthday is March tenth. But her favorite color? Even I figured that one out. It's blue. She wears it all the time. If it's not in her clothes then she wears it on them. Did you notice the earrings?"

He hadn't. He tried to remember and realized he had no idea. Not even what she had on. Marshall shook his head. He thought he was a lost cause too.

"You have to start noticing things about her. Like her perfume, do you like it? If not, then tell her in a way that doesn't come off as you telling her it makes you want to puke on her."

Khan knew better than that.

"You buy her something you like, something to replace what you don't want her to wear...Why aren't you writing this down?"

He opened the pad and began scribbling. He made notes like there was going to be a test later and he didn't want to fail. Because he knew if he did, he'd lose her. After another hour, he was on his way to getting somewhere. He'd even made a list of magazines that Marshall had suggested. And he had purchased tickets to a concert to a band he'd never heard of but Marshall had said she listened to.

Khan left the room feeling like he was going to be able to do this. Now he had to convince her that he wasn't a douche canoe and that he really did love her. He found her in their room asleep on the window seat. She had been crying, and he felt horrible for it.

Picking her up, he put her on the bed. One of the things that Marshall had told him too was that the bed wasn't just for sex. Sometimes it was for holding and talking. Khan didn't know what to say to that, but wrote it down. As soon as he stretched out beside Monica, he understood. He just simply wanted to hold her in his arms. He closed his eyes, content with the way things were going for them, but knew that he had to get down to business. His goal was that his brothers would come to him for advice on wooing the fairer sex. He fell asleep smiling.

~~~

She was alone when she woke. Monica had known that Khan had come up to lay down with her, and she was ready to tell him that she wasn't in the mood for sex. She was, but there was no reason for her to give in so quickly. But he'd held her, and after a few minutes, she heard him give a soft snore. He'd fallen asleep. Trying to be angry with him didn't work, so she closed her eyes and drifted back to sleep.

But waking alone a few hours later had set her off again. How dare he? She wasn't sure how he dared at anything at all, but still stomped around the room gathering her things. She went into the bathroom to have a nice soak when she stopped in her tracks. Someone had been very busy.

There were candles everywhere. On the counter, around the garden tub, and in the windowsill. She touched the rose petals that were around each of the scented candles and marveled at how soft they were. The pink of them matched the candles perfectly. There was also a bottle of wine in a bucket by the tub and two long-fluted glasses.

"I wanted to surprise you." She turned to look at Khan when he spoke. "I was all set to wake you when I realized that I forgot the corkscrew. But you woke before I came back."

She nodded, not sure what else to do. She looked back at the inviting water with the candles that had yet to be lit floating around and more rose petals. It was beautiful.

"Here, let me light these so you can see them. The guy as the store said that they burn for hours." He leaned in the tub and set them to flame. "They smell like lilac. Do you like them?"

"Yes. They're one of my favorite flowers." She could tell that he was nervous, so she sat down on the toilet seat and looked up at him. He was so wonderfully handsome.

"I wanted to make it up to you for being an ass since you met me. I wanted to...I need to make sure you know how much I love you."

"I do. None of this is necessary. I know—"

"But it is. I need this for you." He scrubbed his hand over his face. "I'm not doing this right. I wanted to show you that I'm not a big Neanderthal. I can be, I know, but I'm not always. Especially when it comes to sex."

"You're doing fine." She looked around the room as it soured a little for her. "So you did this because you want me to stay with you because of the sex. That you somehow think that I'm going to—"

He dropped to his knees before her and took her hands. "No. Never that. I meant that I didn't want you to think that I only want sex from you. I want you to hold me, love me, not because you have to because of a twist of the fates, but because you like me enough to give me a chance. I love you, Monica."

When he fumbled on the counter and then reached into the drawer closest to him, she watched him as he swore. It was funny to see the unflappable Khan all messed up about something. He finally seemed to gather whatever it was he needed.

"I wanted to do this after I swept you off your feet and had you begging me for more, but I can't wait. Actually, I'm too terrified to wait any longer." He got up so that he was only resting on one knee and kissed her hand. He did look a little afraid, and she leaned into him and kissed him.

"Whatever it is, we can fix it." She kissed him again when he stayed where he was. "I don't want to live without you either. So just tell me."

He nodded. "Monica, will you marry me?"

The ring he put on her finger was beautiful. She moved her fingers around and let the candlelight catch it, and laughed when it sparkled around the room. She loved the color and thought the chocolate diamond matched his eyes perfectly. She looked up at him. "You didn't have to do this. I love being your mate. If you're doing this to show your dad or because he made you, then you didn't—"

"No, I did this because I should have. A long time ago. And Dad helped me pick it out. He wanted the yellow one, but I thought you'd like this one better." He looked up at her. "You do, don't you? I can take it back and get the yellow one if you want it. Or the white. But—"

She cut him off with her mouth. She lifted her head, looked into his face, and fell in love with him all over. And she told him so. When he kissed her again, he pulled her up off the seat and laughed.

"I guess I could have found a more romantic place to propose to you, but I didn't want you to get away before I asked you." He kissed her again, this time with a little of the hunger she was feeling for him. "If you don't mind, I'd really like to bathe you. I've never done it before and find that I really want to try."

She watched him strip down, and when he was naked, she reached for him. He told her no, this was bath time, and not making love. He told her he had plans for afterward and he didn't want her to mess them up. She giggled as she took off her own clothes.

"Okay, this might have to be both. You're very beautiful without clothes on. With them too, but I think my favorite is like you are right now." He helped her into the tub and settled behind her. "This is very nice."

He'd gotten a large sponge, and he'd washed her back, then her legs. She tried teasing him into making love to her in the tub, but he kept turning her down. When he washed her hair, she made sure she brushed against his hard cock as many times as she could until he set her away from him.

"You, my dear, aren't playing fair. You will behave or I won't give you the rest of your gifts." She sat very still for all of three seconds and lunged at him. "Are you going to make me spank you?"

She moved forward in the tub. He'd gone to so much trouble for her she didn't want to spoil it for him and tell him she would indeed like for him to spank her. Instead, she kissed him. Gently, but with as much love as she could put in it. When she pulled back, she could see that his eyes had darkened. Lust was there, as well as love. She smiled at him and stood up; water ran down her body.

"Take me to bed, Khan. Please?"

Khan

Chapter Thirteen

Khan hated to leave her again, but Walker had said he needed a run and asked him...no, had begged him to go with him. He had been stomping around the house for hours before hand, and when Caitlynne had asked Khan as well to go with him, he finally had.

They'd gone to the very back of the property. Neither of them wanted to be caught with their pants down or as a panther, so this was the best place to be. By the time they'd driven the Jeep out on the pretense of checking out the land, Walker was looking less stressed. Khan didn't want to pry, but he was wondering what had made him so pissy. It wasn't until they were running that his brother reached for him.

"She has to go on an extended trip." It took Khan a second or two to wonder who when Walker continued. *"They want Caitlynne to go to California for a month to see to some training out there that isn't yielding the numbers they had hoped it would."*

"When does she have to leave?" Khan leapt over a log and stopped by a large walnut tree to wait on Walker. *"Are you going with her?"*

"No, I can't. Damn it all to hell. I have to be here in the event Warren needs me." Walker stood beside him for several

133

seconds before he took off again. *"The man is healthier than I am."*

Khan doubted that and said so. *"You took this job, as did she, knowing this might happen. You yourself said that it was best for her not to be put in a kitchen where there were sharp items if you even suggested that she be a nice little housewife."*

Walker growled and Khan laughed. The two of them ran for another twenty minutes before they came to a lake. As they leaned into the water and began lapping at the coolness of it, Walker spoke again.

"She is having a great pregnancy and hasn't really needed anything from me at all."

Khan didn't comment, knowing just how his brother felt about not really being needed.

"She said that she thinks it's a boy. Mom said that there hasn't been a girl born in this family in nearly eight generations. That's a lot of boys."

Khan thought it was longer, but knew that a little girl would probably be very welcome in this family. Overprotected, yes, but well loved. As any child would be.

"This morning when I got up, I was going to make breakfast for Monica and myself and bring it up to the bedroom. But when I rolled out of bed as quietly as I could, she was gone. She'd already gotten up and shooed the cook out of the kitchen so she could make it for me. She's getting much better at cooking. I was really disappointed, myself, in her not needing me." He glanced at his brother as he continued. *"But, her being gone for a month without me? I'm not sure I'd be in any better mood than you. Of course, you do have your own plane. No reason you can't fly out there for a day, then come back."*

Walker's head shot up so quickly that Khan felt his heart leap in his chest. He looked around the area, sure there was a threat. And when his brother attacked him, Khan knew that they both were dead. But Walker only stood over him with his huge fucking paws planted on his chest, then leaned down and licked his face.

"Get off me, you overgrown idiot. What the fuck it wrong with you? I thought we were both dead cats." Walker rolled off him and sat down. *"You want to explain what the fuck that was all about?"*

"You're right."

Khan told him he was always right, but what this time?

"You're right. I can go and visit her anytime I want. She may not be able to get away as much as I'd like to see her, but I can go and be with her when I need to be. So, thank you."

Khan stood up and growled low at his brother. *"Next time, a simple handshake will do. You lick me like that again and I'll break your jaw. And you're welcome."*

This time, when they moved through the forest, it was much more relaxed. They spoke about all kinds of things, mostly their mates and how glad they were that they put up with them. Then they talked about Barr and what his next move might be.

"Caitlynne said it's hard to tell with a man like him. She told me that he's been in and out of institutions for nearly all his life. He was first put in a home when he was five when his sister had been found dead in her crib."

Khan stumbled and stopped moving. *"Did he kill her? Crib implies that she was tiny, less than a year old."*

"She was four months old. The report that Caitlynne was able to find said that he was in a catatonic state when his parents came in the nursery to check on her. Apparently, they

were concerned that she'd not cried at all through the night, but had whimpered once. When they entered the room, I guess it was carnage. Someone, they said, had broken into the house and had murdered the baby, and little Tony had witnessed it."

Khan heard his brother's words, but he also heard more. *"But she doesn't believe it. And neither do you."*

Walker shook his head. *"The autopsy report said her head was crushed, and the bruising around her throat and on her chest was consistent with small hands. When she asked me to look at the report and pictures, even I could see that the hands were tiny, about the size of a five-year-old. He had...Christ, Khan, he'd beaten her with a plastic bat that was found later and then had stood on her little chest at some point. Her death was ruled strangulation."*

"And he wasn't charged."

Walker shook his head.

"His parents covered that murder up like they had the others. The women he had targeted and decided for whatever reason that they were what he wanted. Christ." They were walking back to the Jeep when Khan suddenly stopped and looked around. *"He'll get her, won't he? He'll somehow get Monica and hurt her like he did the others."*

"You can't think like that. We have protection on her twenty-four-seven. She's not stupid and won't let herself get in a predicament that will get her caught." Walker bumped him with his shoulder. *"You have to have faith in the fact that she has all her family around her right now and we won't let anything happen to her."*

Khan hoped not, but he had a feeling that they were only living on borrowed time here. The man was insane, and insane people were hard to reason with and harder to capture.

Caitlynne had told him that yesterday. When they got to the truck, they shifted and dressed.

"If I take you back in a shitty mood and me in a better one, then my ass is toast. I swear to you, Khan, we won't let anything happen to her. And if it does, there won't be an agent working for my wife that won't be out there trying to bring her home. And we will."

Khan hoped so. He would rather die than think about Monica being hurt

~~~

Tony had slept in his car for three nights in a row now, and he wanted a shower. He also wanted food that didn't come to him in a bag. Twice yesterday he'd tried to get someone to fix him a meal, but they had told him to get away. He just wanted somewhere to rest and to eat.

And then there was the blood.

He'd woken yesterday with blood on his clothes again. His face was bruised as well, and he couldn't remember how it had happened. He was sore too, his ribs and his fist like he'd been in a fight. His wallet was fuller, but not by much, and there were credit cards with someone else's name on them. He knew that Jane Matte hadn't given them to him and wondered if he should try to find her to give them back. But he was afraid.

Then there was the added fact that the nightmares were back. He needed to go and get his medication, the ones that helped him sleep and kept the horrible dreams away. They were in his apartment, but whenever he tried to remember where he had lived, his nose would bleed and he'd get sick. Not even his driver's license was helpful. He couldn't read the address. Just his name and that he lived in Virginia.

He looked at the house he'd noticed last night. He had a feeling that Monica was in it, and he was going to go in and ask her why she'd murdered his parents. Tony had been very proud of his reasonable conversation with himself just the other day. He'd figured out that she had been playing him all the time, and when he hadn't been able to find her quickly enough, she'd killed his father and mother, and now he was an orphan.

Maybe at thirty, he wasn't a real orphan and wouldn't be going to one of those work prisons that his mother had always threatened him with. Every time he'd been bad, done one of the things that got him into "deep shit," as she'd called it, she would tell him how he was going to end up killing her.

When the woman had come out to get her paper, he got out of the car. He had to wait another few minutes for the school bus to stop in front of her house and for the man to leave. It wasn't the same as the one that had been in her hotel room, but he knew what kind of woman Monica was. Slut. Whore. Cunt. Names his mother had used to speak about some of the women she was on committees with. When the man got into his car, Tony made his move.

The stop sign was right in front of him, and when the man stopped at it, pausing just long enough, Tony shot him in the head. Scrambling over to the driver's side, he'd had to lift his head off the horn and put the car in park. He also took the keys. The man wasn't the same, but it didn't matter now.

Moving toward the house, he looked at the keys in his hand and tried to find the one that would let him in the house that Monica was in. He had to try twice before he found the one he had wanted. The door opened quietly and he slipped inside.

The house was messy with kids' toys and laundry baskets. She wasn't in the first room he'd come to, nor the second. He found her in the kitchen washing the dishes and singing to the radio. He hated the extra noise and turned it off.

She turned toward him with a smile, and when she saw him, she opened her mouth to scream. He shoved the gun in her mouth. That shut her up.

"I want to know who that man was, Monica. You should know better than to try and see other people when you've said you were going to marry me." The woman shook her head and cried. "You have to stop that. I hate crying. I hate it, hate it, hate it."

He pulled the trigger when she made noises that made his head hurt. Someone had made noises like that before. All the time. He had done something to stop it. He had… Tony stepped over her body to sit at the table.

His nose was bleeding again, and he found a cloth and put it to his face. When that didn't help, he went to the refrigerator and filled the towel with ice and held it on his nose. He laid his head on the table and tried to think calm words again. But they were gone.

All his words he'd had to remember were now words like "dead," "blood," "bullets," and "Monica." Before when he'd thought of his Monica, he had her in the calm words list. Now she was in a list that he didn't like. But he'd done what he'd needed and made her pay. Getting up, he walked to her again and looked at her eyes.

They were brown. Monica's were a deep purple, almost black. He put his finger to her eye and moved it around, hoping for a contact or some other way to explain why she now had brown eyes. When nothing helped, he sat back on the floor and leaned against the counter.

"It's not Monica." He kicked the woman in the ribs. "Where is she? What did you do with her? I saw her here yesterday. Where is she?"

Of course she didn't answer and Tony stood up. He started in the basement, went through the house quickly, and was looking in the bedrooms when the sirens sounded. It took him several minutes to figure out which side of the house he was on to find a window that worked for him.

He glanced out the upper pink bedroom and saw the three cruisers. He noticed right away that they weren't coming to the house, but down the street a few feet. When the ambulance pulled up, he walked to the kitchen to see if fake Monica had called them. She was still dead.

Tony was starving and went to the refrigerator again. There were leftovers, which he hated, and some lunch meats. He made himself five thick sandwiches and stuffed them and all the bottled water she had into a large grocery bag he found behind the door to the pantry. Here, he took some pudding snacks, as well as a few cans of pop-off-lidded soups. He was walking out the back door ten minutes after the first siren sounded.

He wasn't happy that Monica had managed to elude him. And he had a feeling that the woman in the house had been a plant to throw him off her scent. Tony went to his car and put all his food in the back seat. He was eating a sandwich when he pulled into the street, and turned when the policeman there directing traffic told him to. He wondered what had happened.

By the time he was at the mall, he had a pounding headache. Tony wasn't sure why he'd gone there, but he had to crawl into the back seat to rest again. That's when he found the food.

He tried to remember where he'd gotten it and his head started hurting again. They were good; he ate one while he was lying down, and the water was good and cold. He didn't have a spoon, so he drank the pudding out of the cup like a juice and then closed his eyes. He wondered who was caring for him.

The food notwithstanding, there had been blankets just the other day. And then there had been a stockpile of small containers of instant coffee. He wasn't allowed coffee and had no way of heating up any water. He'd thrown them out before going to…

The bloodied rag in his hand had made him think that he'd had another nose bleed, but the ice in the thing made him scared. Where had the ice come from, and what had happened to make him so upset that his nose would bleed?

He heard voices and tensed up. He didn't want to ever hear voices again, and when someone slammed a car door next to him, he nearly leapt out of his car at them. Tony laid there for several minutes waiting for his heart to stop pounding before he sat up. That's when he saw the newspaper under his wiper.

Getting out, he looked around. It had snowed since he'd come here. He couldn't even tell that he'd been here for only a short amount of time. But the paper was in a plastic bag and it wasn't harmed. When he opened it, a sheet of paper fell out and he read it. The newspaper wanted him to have this and hoped that he would consider taking a subscription. Yeah, right.

When he opened it up, there was a huge headline that read, "Barr Couple Murdered in Their Own Home." He got back in the back seat and read the entire article. Then he read it again.

He wasn't mentioned. Going to the obituaries page, he found both their names on the full page write-ups. He wasn't even a "special friend," or even a footnote. Scanning the article on the first page again, he tore the paper into pieces and tossed them out of his car.

"Why does no one care that my parents are dead to me? Why? Why?" He looked around the empty containers and fast-food bags in the back seat. "They don't care. Monica should have told them that I was their son. She should have made them put me in the paper. Somebody should have noticed that I was gone."

Closing his eyes, he tried to sleep. Sometimes when he was able to do that, his headaches would go away and he'd be fine. He wanted to be fine. He needed to be fine so he could find Monica and make her pay. He decided that when he woke, he was going to go and find the cop lady, Bowding, and make her tell him. He frowned, thinking that the name wasn't quite right, but he'd find her anyway.

How hard could it be to find a pretty cop like her in this town? Women like her had to hang out at the hair dressers or something. Smiling and feeling in control for the first time in ages, since he'd decided to marry Monica, he let sleep take him. Soon, he thought lastly, soon they would all know that you just didn't hurt Anthony Barr and walk away.

Chapter Fourteen

Monica watched the news again. They had been running the same feed for over three hours, and she wanted to make sure what she was seeing was actually there. When Caitlynne came home from work, she had her sit down with her and watch it.

"I've heard nothing but this all day. That poor couple and those children. What will they do now? They had no other relatives."

Monica had heard that too. But when the news team put up the pictures again, she asked Caitlynne to look at them.

"I know, so young. The woman had just gotten her children off to school. They think that the man had been killed first and the woman—"

"Look at her," Monica snapped. "That woman could be me but for the eyes." Picking up the remote, Caitlynne rewound the feed. Monica had tried that earlier and had ended up changing the channels three times before she set the stupid thing away from her and watched it live.

"I don't know." Caitlynne peered closer, then sat back and looked at her. "You think Barr did this?"

Monica nodded. "The woman has the same color hair as me and the same…same everything. You said he was in town. Maybe he thought I was there for whatever reason. Maybe he really is nuts like you said and he is going to kill more people until—"

"Calm down." Khan had entered the room and shook her shoulder. "I need you to calm down and talk to me. I can feel your fear like it's my own. You're safe here. I won't let anyone hurt you."

"Khan, I think she might be right." He looked over at Caitlynne and asked her about what. "The woman on the news, the one that was killed in her house and her husband in his car? I think Monica is right; they do look a great deal alike. I'm going to make a couple of calls. I'll be right back."

When she left the room, Khan sat down in front of her. She took his warm hands into her cold ones. She was terrified out of her mind, but took several deep breaths to calm herself. "He thought it was me. I don't know why I think that, but the second I saw her picture, I knew it was him." He sat on the couch beside her. "That woman died because that man is a sick son of a bitch and he's out there." She heard him laugh and she looked up at him, ready to tear him apart for laughing at her.

"I was thinking you needed comfort, that you might be thinking this is your fault, but you're a hell cat, aren't you?"

"I don't know what you're talking about." She tried to pull away from him and he pulled her back. "If you're going to make fun of me, let me go. I can go and find someone else that will appreciate me and what I'm trying to do."

"Oh I appreciate you all right. You're one hell of a woman and I love you. But if you think I'm letting you go find someone else, you're off your rocker. You belong to me to make fun of."

She slugged him in the arm jokingly and laid her head on his chest, frowning. "What if I'm right? What if he starts killing women who look like me? We're going to have to step this up or we might be in for a mass murder situation. More than we were before."

"Caitlynne will figure it out. Maybe he left more clues behind and she can find him faster. Anything is possible. The guy has been killing and hurting people for days now and he leaves a little more behind every time."

He had too. Just yesterday they had connected him to another murder, this time of a clerk in a store. And there had been video, but no sound of the entire incident. They had been talking, he and the clerk, and suddenly, there was a gun in Tony's hand. When he started waving it around in what appeared to be an agitated state, the man dropped to his knees and looked to be praying. Tony simply shot him. Then he did the strangest thing. He began beating his head with the gun.

Then he walked around picking up items and putting them into a bag and walked out of the store. Caitlynne said that it looked as if he had gotten coffee, of all things, and a great deal of it.

She was still lying with her head on Khan's chest when Caitlynne returned. She had one of the other men with her, one of the guards that had been sent to watch her today. Caitlynne didn't look very happy.

"You're right. His DNA was found at the scene. It had come up as a match, but they wanted to run it again because of how far this one was from the last murder. They think he went inside to get something to eat, he must be running low on money, and she tried to stop him. Apparently, he had made himself at home and rummaged through the house before he left. Drops of his blood were found throughout the house, including the children's rooms." Caitlynne nodded to the man who had entered with her. "This is Karl. He's going to continue your shooting lessons today. I have to go to this crime scene and see what I can find out. We're running out of time."

Monica had nearly shut down when she'd heard that he'd been in the children's rooms. She wondered if he had been looking for them to harm them. She wondered what, if anything, could be done to help these children get on with their lives. She stood up suddenly and looked around at the three people there. "I need to be alone. I know that someone has to watch over me, but I need to…really need to be in a quiet place to think. I'm sorry, but…" She looked at the man. "I'm sorry, but we can do this later? Right now I need—" She ran to the bathroom with her hand over her mouth. She was going to be sick right now. By the time she threw up a few times, she heard the door behind her open and close. She thought it was Caitlynne, but when Khan spoke, she moaned.

"I have some crackers for you. And I've got something here that Walker left in the event this got to be too much for you. I think you should take it." She reached for the crackers, but left the little pink pill in his palm. "I don't want to have to make you take this, but I will. You're not going to be able to help when they need you if you're too ill. I love you, babe. You need to rest."

"He killed those people for no other reason than he thought she looked like me." She took the pill, put it in her mouth, and swallowed. He handed her a glass of water, which she sipped.

"Did I ever tell you about the time that Walker and I got into trouble because he wanted to have sex with this older woman and I tried to stop him?" She cocked her brow at him and he smiled. "It's my version of the story and you'll believe me because you love me. Anyway, he wanted to have sex with this woman and I told him it was a bad idea."

"And how old was this older woman?" She knew that he'd been the one who wanted the sex and Walker was the one trying to keep him from getting into trouble. She had no doubt that there were plenty of stories like this one where he was the innocent bystander.

"Oh very old to a couple of barely teenage boys. She was nearing to dotage at twenty-five." She laughed as he continued. "She lived near the land that my parents had. The original acres to the property we have back home. A lot less than now. Anyway, she lived near us and baked the best cinnamon rolls in seven counties. They were tender and soft. Just big enough to fit in your hand. And as warm as the sunshine on a nice May day."

"Are you talking about the rolls or the woman's breasts? Sounds to me you were a horny kid looking for a quick lay." He grinned at her and told her to hush. She yawned and he picked her up off the floor and held her.

"Stop interrupting me. Where was I? Oh, yeah. Her rolls. She would bake them every week and send some to our house as a gift to my mom. Mom would help her in the gardens, and we got warm rolls for it. But I...Walker wanted more."

Monica felt her body begin to relax, and she snuggled into Khan's warmth as he talked. His words seemed to slur, but she no longer cared about the woman or her cinnamon roll-flavored breasts. When Khan laughed, she tried to look up at him, but he too was blurry.

"I think you pinked my pill." No, that wasn't right. "You put something in my pinked nipple." She knew that wasn't right either, but his laughter made her smile. She tried to tell him good night, but was pretty sure it hadn't come out that way. He was still laughing when she felt the bed beneath her. Tired beyond belief, she let him cover her up and slipped away.

~~~

When Khan woke, he nearly came up off the bed. His cock was in the warmest place in the world. Looking down, he saw that Monica had him deep in her mouth and she was thoroughly enjoying herself. He curled his fingers into her hair and lifted her head to look at him.

"You certainly know how to wake a man." Her grin was positively evil. "Are you going to give me a taste of you as well?"

She sat up and looked at him. Her breasts were flushed with need and her nipples were hard peaks on the tips. He wanted to sit up, take them into his mouth, and suckle them. But she had his shaft in her hand and was doing delightful things to it.

"You don't like me waking you this way? I thought all men enjoyed their cock serviced first thing in the morning." He was going to have to show her tomorrow how a man liked to wake up. "I want to suck you until you come."

"I want to drink from you. Turn around and we can both get what we want." He helped her turn so that she was over his head. "That's it, baby."

She leaned down, took his cock in her mouth, and he pulled her hips down so that he could feast on her. She was so wet already that he only lapped at her thighs to gather her cream. As soon as he pulled her closer and licked along her seam, she moaned around his cock. He felt it all the way to his toes.

Every bit of her was exposed for him. With her thighs spread over his head, she was as open as he'd ever had her. When he cupped her ass and ran his fingers along that seam, she danced over his mouth and more of her juices flowed from her. He knew he could scare her if he touched her like this, so he was content to eat her and drink from her.

Tilting his head sideways, he was able to see her. She was bobbing up and down on his cock so quickly that he knew that he was going to come down her throat at any second. Sliding his fingers along her ass again, he waited for her to tense up, but she was too involved in what she was doing. When he pressed against her tight rings, he felt her stiffen and took her clit back into his mouth until she relaxed again. He did this twice more before he was able to slide his finger into her.

She nipped at his cock and then pulled one of his balls into her mouth. Crying out against her, he came, fucking her mouth as hard as he could while pumping in and out of her with both his tongue and finger. As soon as he felt her tighten around him, he reached between her soft nether lips, pinched her clit, and was rewarded with her scream of release and a flood of her essences.

While she was still reeling from her climax, her body jerking and convulsing, he adjusted her so that she lay beside him. When she smiled at him, he rolled over on top of her and laced his fingers into her. Kissing her, he centered himself over her, and she wrapped her legs around his hips.

"I want to make love to you." He slid deep into her wet sheath and moaned. "Hot and tight. I love you wrapped around me."

Moving slowly, he watched her face. She was beautiful when she was coming, and he loved watching her face as she enjoyed them together. Moving his head down her body, he stopped at her breast and teased her nipples with his tongue and teeth. When she tried to get him deeper and to go faster, he slowed more.

"This is my turn."

She growled at him.

"That's very sexy, but I want to take my time with you. You're always so impatient to get to the end and forget to enjoy the uphill climb." When he moved into her again, he made sure he twisted, and smiled when she cried out. "You love me, don't you."

It wasn't a question, but she answered him. "Yes. Very much so. Please, Khan, I want to come. So badly. Help me."

"I have to tell you something. Some of it you might have figured out, but I need to tell you something important." She nearly had him forget what he was telling her when she lifted her legs higher around him and hooked her ankles. "You never play fair."

"Neither do you. Tell me or fuck me. I'm dying here." He laughed, and she moaned when he gave her three quick strokes with his cock. "Please."

"I'm wealthy." She looked at him and laid back down. "I had some money before, but after Walker and Caitlynne got married, she set each of us up with a nice, fat account and paid off all our debt."

"Okay. Is that it? I don't care how much money you have. I have none, so we balance each other out. But if you don't give me what I want, I'm going to be a widow and have all your thousands anyway."

"Millions." She stopped moving; her breath caught. "I was a millionaire because of my business before she had given us money. I was in the process of selling it off when she and Walker met. When I found out about the money and after the sale of my business, I tried to give it back to her and she said no. Did you know she was a billionaire?"

"This is her house?" He nodded. "I thought it...I don't know, came with the job she has with the CIA."

He nuzzled her breast and took her nipple into his mouth before he lifted his head again. "I want you to know that no matter what it is you want to do, where you want to live, that you'll never have to worry about money. Ever."

When he moved in her now, she didn't move. He didn't mind and knew that he could bring her back to the point they'd been before he'd spoken. He had needed to tell her because of the conversation he'd had with Walker about his new mate.

Her climax rolled through her and she grabbed his shoulders as he nipped at her throat. When he scraped his teeth along the vein, she flipped him to his back and sat up.

"I want you to know that if you do this to me again during sex, I'll do the opposite of what I did to you this morning. Understand?"

Khan rolled her back to her back and pounded hard through several strokes before he lifted his head. "You are my mate, now and forever. I never want you to worry. Ever."

Lowering his head, he bit her. Her scream of pleasure brought him over the tight edge he'd been near since he'd entered her. He felt her lick his own throat and tilted his head to let her have him. When her teeth sank hard and successfully drew blood, he came again, emptying himself of not only his climax, but of everything he was.

Sealing the wounds at her throat, he felt her tongue do the same to him. He lifted his head and looked down at her. She was looking a little pissed, so he kissed her again. He rolled them so that she was spread over him and he was on his back.

"Why did you tell me like that? Were you afraid I'd run away from you or something?"

He laughed. "No. I told you like that because I didn't want you to ever think that you have to worry. Walker said you asked Caitlynne if I was going to lose my job being here with you."

She sat up and rested her chin on her hand. "I don't know that much about you. Hardly anything. Like, what is your birthday?"

"July twenty-fourth. Yours is March tenth. And Marshall told me. But that's all I know too. We should spend some time together seeing the Capitol and hanging out together." He laid her head back on his chest. "After a nap. You've worn me out."

Chapter Fifteen

They enjoyed the day. Monica had never been to DC before and she'd not seen much more of the city than Caitlynne's back yard and house since she'd come here with Caitlynne over three weeks ago. And Khan was being a wonderful tour guide. He told her that for his business, he'd traveled a great deal and had seen a lot of capitals.

"I had a very nice law firm. We worked all sorts of cases and had a few high profile trials. During that time, I did a lot of traveling for myself. I had to get away at the time. Then after Roseann...after her, I simply sold out and went back home to lick my wounds."

Monica nodded. She knew about licking wounds. She had been doing the same thing since Tony had decided that she was for him. They stopped at a little restaurant and had some wonderful gyros and fries. She couldn't believe how much she was able to eat nowadays.

"It's the extra energy you're burning."

She flushed.

"Not just with the sex, but as the partial panther you've become. We burn hotter, and though you can't shift, you're still burning a great many calories. Wait until you're pregnant. You'll really pack it away."

Her fork stopped halfway to her mouth. "Do you want children? With me? I don't know what sort of mother to be to panthers. Do they require anything different?"

"Yes. They eat raw steak at birth and they can chew your breast off when you nurse them." Her fork dropped and he burst out laughing. "I'm kidding. No. They're normal babies until they reach around thirteen. Some can shift early, like my mom, but mostly it's around puberty. You should have seen the look on your face."

Monica threw her napkin at him. He smiled at her gently and took her hand. She loved it when he looked at her like that.

"And in answer to your question, yes, I want to have children with you. As many as you're willing to have. I want as many as my mother had, but you'll be the one that has to carry them, and I don't want anything to happen to them."

They finished their meal and went back out into the cold. He took her to one of the nicer shops on a side street and told the lady behind the counter they had an appointment. She apparently knew Khan.

"Khan, it's been an age. Where have you been hiding yourself? Are you buying for that special lady in your life?"

Monica looked at him, wanting to both leave and kill him at the same time.

"No. This is for Monica. Monica, I'd like you to meet Alice Combs. Alice, my mate. My mother said she talked to you this morning and you knew what I wanted." When the woman nodded and walked away, he turned to her. "I buy things in here for my mom. Ask her. I buy her a formal dress that she wears to the charity thing they have for Panthers without Parents. I do it every year."

She believed him, but didn't want to let him off the hook that easily. She walked up to him and cupped his cock in her hand, and he stood very still. When she gave it a sharp but short tug, he groaned. "You want to keep this impressive appendage, then I would suggest that you never take me anywhere that you took that bitch. Understand?" He nodded. "And for the record, when I see her, I'm tearing her eyes out."

When she removed her hand, he pulled her to him for a hard kiss. "And so you know, I'm going to let you. And she would never come in here. This place is owned by the woman that you just met and not a big brand name shop. Roseann was big on names."

The woman was pushing a rack. On it were several gowns and a few wraps. Monica looked at Khan. He only shrugged. She was going to murder him in his sleep as soon as she got him alone.

"Warren and Marshall have invited us to the Christmas Ball at the White House tonight. It's a private affair, they said, but it's formal. I wanted you to be able to dress up. So I had Mom call Alice and had her find you a few things to try on." He took her hand and kissed it. "Besides, I thought it would be a nice break for you to think about something besides Barr for a little while."

She looked at the dresses hanging there and back at him. "These are very expensive, even I can tell that. I can't let you—"

He kissed her. "You can and you will. Besides, I've taken the advice of a very wealthy woman and had everything I own put into your name as well, Monica Bowen, but we're going to take care of that as soon as we can get this other mess taken care of."

She thought he was hiding something from her, but didn't know what. When Alice showed her the fitting room, she followed. There were things there already laid out for her as well.

"Corrine didn't know for sure what size you were, so I put several different sizes in here for you. Some of them go with specific dresses so we'll look at those if we get that far." Alice lifted her hair up off her neck and twisted it into a sharp bun. "You have such a lovely neck. I would think that wearing your hair up sort of like this would be just lovely."

She fussed with some of the items and handed her a pretty bra and panty set. Then she handed her a robe. Alice told her that she'd have her put the dresses to her skin to see which ones suited her before she tried them on.

"But I must admit, I believe that there is only one dress that'll do for you. It's the cranberry one that has the... Let me get rid of Khan, and you and I will play. He mentioned shopping for his tux as well." She disappeared, then returned a short time later. "I told him that when we found a dress, he wasn't to peek until you got to the ball. He said that he would try to promise that, but wasn't making any kind of guarantees. He loves you very much."

Monica nodded. "And I love him as well. But I don't...I don't want you to be insulted, but this is going to very expensive for him. I know that he says he can afford it, but I don't want him to spend money on me for a dress when I'm sure I could borrow one of the other ladies'." She fingered the cranberry dress. It was so beautiful, but she was afraid of the cost.

Alice tisked at her. She looked like she had a secret too. "When I first started this business, nearly ten years ago now, Khan and his mother were my very first customers. He wanted a dress for her for some event and I barely had enough money after buying this place to pay the payment much less purchase the money for the material needed to make a dress I could already see Corrine in. He made the arrangements to pick it up, even inviting me to the hotel where she was staying to help her put it on correctly. He said he'd pay for such service. And he did." She took the dress off the padded hanger and handed it to Monica. "Before he left, he handed me some money and his business card. He said that he knew it was expensive to run a shop and wanted to make sure that his mother looked good. He winked at me, then left. I looked down at the cash in my hand."

The dress slid over her head and pooled at her feet like it had been lengthened just for her. When she looked in the three-sided mirror, she watched, mesmerized as Alice zipped up the back, the dress seeming to mold to her body. Even the bodice seemed to have been made for her ample bosom. "How much did he give you?" Monica asked the woman smiling at her as she held up her hair. "He gave you enough to run this place, didn't he?"

"Yes, for a very long time. I will never forget him or his mother. They have been and always will be the best people I've ever met. And you should know that he will never hurt you and will love you for the rest of his days."

Monica looked at herself in the mirror. She almost didn't know the person staring back at her. Her eyes were darker than they'd ever been, cheeks flushed with rosy health, and her lips, even after being kissed by Khan so long ago, looked fuller and more lush.

"I think this is the one."

Alice nodded.

"I've never seen a more beautiful dress in all my life. Thank you for this." She hugged Alice, then stepped back to look at the shoes she'd brought in for her to wear. They made her several inches taller, and when she'd lifted the dress, her legs looked fabulous. Monica couldn't stop looking at it.

"It's not just the dress, my dear. Even though I made it, I can honestly say that I doubt anyone would have been able to make it look even half that good. It's as if it was made for you."

~~~

The limo pulled up in front of the White House at a quarter till seven. They were supposed to be there at seven, and Monica was sure that they were running behind. Caitlynne had had to answer the phone seven times, and Walker had to assure his mother numerous times that his dad was wearing a tux and not his jeans and t-shirt. They were a group to reckon with. Even Dylan had come up for the event.

Each of the Bowen men had on a tuxedo. And each of them looked good enough to eat. She decided that if a woman had to wear heels and an expensive gown to mingle with people she didn't know, these were the men she wanted to do it with. And Caitlynne looked amazing. She remembered the conversation again that they'd had when Caitlynne was having her makeup done.

"Isn't it great what they can do with maternity clothes these days? Alice said I should show off my baby, not hide it away. I didn't tell her that I'd been having a hard time simply putting on clothes. I was so tired all the time, and I'm only six months pregnant." She looked at her in the mirror over her vanity. "Do you know what it is? The doctor doesn't have a clue."

"Yes. Do you really want to know? Because once I tell you, I can't un-tell you."

Caitlynne bit her lip then nodded.

"It's a boy, and he's full blooded panther. He's going to be big, so you'd better be resting."

Caitlynne finished her makeup and sat down. She looked pole-axed, yet very happy. Monica smiled at her when she turned from the vanity.

"I know that Walker said he'd be happy either way, but the thought of trying to raise a girl terrified me. I don't know anything at all about being a girly girl, and it would be my luck she'd be one." She looked around the room. "It won't be long now. The end of April."

"You'll make a wonderful mother. And Walker a great dad. You two have so much family around you that you can't help but do wonderfully. And the baby will be so spoiled."

Caitlynne nodded.

"I envy you. Khan said that it's not time for us yet. I'm not sure when it will be."

"He means you're not what they refer to as 'in-heat.' I know it sounds weird, but that's what Walker called it. He said it's a quarterly thing for us. I don't know how they can tell, but they can." She looked at her with a smile. "We were so happy to get started on a baby. You'll be that way for an entire week, and you simply cannot get enough sex."

Monica wondered how that was possible since she couldn't get enough now. When they were told by the maid that the car was here, they both put on their capes. Neither of them had wanted their mates to see the dresses they had on. And now here they were.

Monica knew she'd picked well when Khan growled low as he buried his face in her neck. She nearly knocked him to the floor when he nipped gently at her flesh. He lifted his head from her and looked deeply into her eyes.

"Any man that touches you tonight will be dead within the hour. Remember that when someone asks you to dance." She believed him. He looked positively feral, and she had never felt so loved in her life.

The president and Marshall met them in the main hall. They were both dressed in tuxedos as well. When Marshall reached for her, she remembered what Khan had said and nearly backed away. He laughed at her.

"He won't mind tonight. I've helped him with a special treat for you." He put his arm around her waist, but she did notice that he didn't actually touch her skin. "Come on, everyone. Everything is ready."

The room they were led to was decorated beautifully. There was a huge Christmas tree as well as a great many gifts under it. She walked to the tree to see the tiny white ornaments, and that's when she noticed the altar.

She looked at Khan, then back at the man who walked toward her. This wasn't a dinner party after all. Khan held her hand as he led her to the front of the room. When they stood before his family, she started to cry.

"I know that some of you knew what was happening tonight, and I want to thank you for helping me make this happen." He looked at her. "Monica Preston, will you become my bride tonight and allow me to spend the rest of my life making you happy and keeping you safe?"

The second ring he slipped onto her finger was a band that was encircled in diamonds. These were all white with a single chocolate one on top. He kissed her again and then led her to the altar. They were getting married.

When Corrine and George stood with them as their best man and matron of honor, Monica knew for the rest of her days she would remember this day as the most wonderful one in her life. She looked up at Khan. "I didn't say yes." He looked at her wide-eyed, and she nearly laughed. "You've been handling me again, and we had a talk about this, remember?"

"Yes, but I—"

"No buts. You told me just this morning that we would make sure that we discussed any big decisions and not make them without consulting the other." She looked over at George who looked ready to bust his buttons on his jacket. "Would you consider this a big decision, George?"

"Yes," he told her with a strained voice full of humor. "I would say this rates right up there with one of the biggest."

"Dad, you're not helping."

She turned him to look at her when he continued to glare at his dad. "You think you need help with me, big boy?" He shook his head then leaned down to her ear. When he nipped at it hard, she knew she'd gone too far.

"No. You don't need help. Because if you don't stop this right now, I'm going to make you wish you had." He kissed her on the mouth. "Marry me?"

"Well of course I will. I'm so glad you asked." The wedding proceeded with everyone laughing right along with them.

It was a grand affair, one she knew that forever would be the greatest day in both their lives. The staff at the White House had gone all out for their wedding feast and by the time the wedding cake was rolled out, she was so full she thought she'd need a cart to take her out.

Along with tomato bisque, there was rare roast beef with new potatoes, green beans with ham, and grilled onions. Grilled asparagus with butter was accompanied by rolls so fluffy that biting into them was heavenly. Fresh fruit and small almond cookies graced the table as well as center pieces made from marzipan that had been shaped into small Christmas trees decorated with tiny candy canes and little brightly-colored balls.

The cake, however, was a masterpiece. Three tiers of white frosting that were decorated for the coming spring. Flowers and butterflies with the same cranberry of her dress, cherry trees with small blossoms ready to open. But it was the artwork across the bottom that had her smile. Panthers ran around the entire cake, chasing and jumping over logs and the forest grounds. And in one corner were a white Bengal tiger and a large orange one as well. She kissed both men on the cheek when she saw them there with her family.

"We couldn't just let the black cats have all the fun. Besides," Warren told her with a hug, "you're as much part of our family as the rest of them. I do hope you enjoyed your wedding day. Khan worked very hard on pulling this off."

"I did. Very much so. And thank you for everything. Not many people can say that they were married at the White House." And, of course, she couldn't either. There were strict rules about this sort of thing. So they had said it was simply a party to celebrate their day.

As the band started playing, she went to find her husband. It sounded strange to say that and couldn't wait to be able to sign her name officially as Monica Bowen. She found Khan in the rose garden with his brothers.

As soon as she kissed them all and they welcomed her to the family, they left her and Khan alone. He pulled her into his arms and began dancing with her in the moonlight. It was cold, but he kept her very warm.

"I love you very much."

She smiled at him when he told her.

"I have one more gift for you."

"You've done so much for me today. I love you very much."

He kissed her again and reached into his pocket. "It's been in my family for generations. I think for about fourteen or so." He took the necklace out of the long box and had her turn around. "Every leader of the family has a small stone added to it. The addition will mean something to him and he gives it to his mate so she can remember him."

He showed her the small stone that was his. It was a bright amethyst as purple, he told her, as her eyes when she looked at him.

The necklace was on a braided chain, chain mail, he told her, so that if it were ever worn when the wearer shifted, it wouldn't break as easily. The pendent was a beautiful carved panther. Under his face was a large decorative "B" for the family name. The stones were balanced on either side and she noticed that hers was the only purple one. The one opposite of hers was a moonstone, white with caramel-colored veins running through it.

Just after midnight, they went back to Walker and Caitlynne's home. She and Khan were to go to a hotel, but they ended up at the house with everyone else when Caitlynne got word of another murder. They wanted to be close in the event that Barr wasn't finished for the night.

"We have to do something. He's not going to stop."

Monica agreed with Caitlynne.

"Tomorrow. Tomorrow, we're going to sit down with a team and we're going to figure out a way to find him and bring him in. Short of that, we're going to have to put you somewhere safe. Where he won't find you ever."

Neither she nor Khan wanted to go into hiding.

Kathi S. Barton

Chapter Sixteen

Tony lay where he was for several minutes. He could move. He just didn't have a clue where he was. Or for that matter how he had gotten there. It was bright out, he knew that much. And he was out of doors because he was freezing cold. Rolling over so that he was face up, he opened his eyes slowly.

He was between two buildings. An alley, he supposed. There was something near him, blue and metal; he looked at it and realized it was a dumpster. One much like they had at one of the homes he'd been in. Tony sat up. There was snow thick on his body. So he had been out there for some time. Either that or someone had piled it over him. He looked around more and realized that he'd been wherever he was for some time because there were no prints leading up to his body. After brushing off the snow, he saw that, once again, he was covered in blood.

"No, no, no, no." Closing his eyes didn't help; he still saw it. Looking at himself again, he saw that not only his clothes were covered, his hands were as well. Burying them in the snow, he tried to wash it all away to see if he'd injured himself and found that, while he did have a few cuts, nothing to explain the amount of blood he had on him. That's when he noticed the knife.

It wasn't like the one his mother used when she cooked. This one had a handle that he knew the blade fit inside of. He didn't pick it up immediately, but studied it. The serrated edge was covered in blood and things he wasn't going to think about. He knew a little about switchblades, enough to see that this one was an out the front type of knife and longer than most. The blade itself looked to be at least nine inches long. A custom job, he thought.

Looking around, he reached down and picked it up. It wasn't heavy like he'd expected, and the handle had carving in it. Without having to wash off all the blood first, he would say it was of a skull. The blood added to its macabre look. He pushed the tab on the side and the blade slid easily into the handle.

He'd been bad again.

Tony leaned back against the dumpster behind him and felt the pain of his headache coming on. He didn't know what he'd done, but something that had him covered in blood. Yesterday was a blur and last night was gone. He lay there and cried. He just wanted to show Monica that she'd hurt him.

Standing up, he pulled his coat around him. He had no idea what his face looked like so he reached down, grabbing hands full of snow, and scrubbed his face with it. When it dripped red from his hands, he did it several more times until it rained down clear. Stuffing his hands in his pockets, he stepped out of the alley.

There weren't that many cars around, but he didn't recognize where he was. He tried to find a street sign, but there didn't seem to be any where he was, so he started walking. He wondered what day it was.

There were several papers in trashcans along the way. But each of them had a different date on them. Frustrated, he turned to the first person he saw and asked him what the date was. The man grunted at him and kept walking. Tony was half tempted to pull out the bloodied knife and ram it though the rude man's heart, but he didn't. That would get him into trouble again.

The next person he asked told him it was the twenty-second. He thanked him and went back to the trashcan. There was one newspaper in it for today. Taking it out. He started to enter a coffee shop and saw that it was occupied with several men in blue. He wasn't going to get himself into trouble if they saw what was on his shirt. Moving down the block, he entered another alley and sat near another dumpster, this one rust-covered, and read the first page of the paper.

The word "MANHUNT" screamed across the headline. He read the article, hoping it was about his parents and maybe this time someone had finally remembered him. But it talked about how there had been a string of murders and it had begun with his parents. Reading the entire article twice, he tossed it away.

"Why hasn't she told them about me? Why is she not telling the police that I'm their son?" He kicked out at the paper again and reached to grab it up. There she was. Right there.

"Mr. and Mrs. Khan Bowen were married last night, bringing one of the most eligible bachelors to his knees." Tony looked at the picture of the man and woman before continuing on with the post. "Monica Preston Bowen, bride to the fortune five-hundred topper, was wearing a cranberry gown handmade for her by Alice Combs of *Alice on the James Specialty Shop*. The couple will be residing at the home of his brother, another topper on the list of rich men, and his lovely wife Caitlynne Bowen, who were married late last year."

The article droned on, but Tony stopped reading. How could she do this to him? How could she just ignore the fact that he and his mother were planning this big wedding for this month? And wouldn't she want to honor his parents even though someone had murdered them? Tony got up and paced.

She really was a slut. As soon as he couldn't find her, she'd gone off and found herself someone else just like that? Apparently, she had never loved him at all. She'd been using him. He didn't like to be used. He didn't like it one bit. He was going to find her and tell her that too. He was going to find her right now.

Walking along the streets, he looked for his car. He didn't have a clue where he'd left it and was getting very afraid that someone had taken it thinking it was the car that Bowen woman had showed on the news. He was just stepping by a bar when he heard his name. Not his first name, but his last. He entered, but kept back in the darkened corner and ordered a beer.

He held it in his hand, not touching the nasty stuff, looking at each patron there. He didn't know any of them and was ready to leave when he glanced up at the television hanging crookedly over the back of the bar.

"...last night. This is the fourth murder like this one in just under two weeks. The police are working tightly with the CIA as well as other bureaus to bring this crime spree to an end. According to the police, they are looking for the same man. They said that he is in his mid-thirties with dark blond hair. He will be strong and he is considered armed and dangerous. Here is a sketch of the man that a witness has given us."

Tony looked around the room again, this time not looking to see if he knew anyone, but if they recognized him from the drawing. He was the man in the drawing. Including the scar on his lip he'd gotten when he was a child. He threw money on the bar and backed to the door. No one turned, no one said anything, but he moved as if every eye in the place were on him. As soon as he stepped out, he took off running. He ran until he couldn't run any longer.

They thought he was the murderer. That he'd killed four people. Who would have told them such a thing? Who was this lying witness that was working to get him framed for something he'd not done? Terrified out of his mind, he tried to think. His head was pounding and he reached into his pocket and touched the gun with his left hand while his right wrapped around the knife. With a sudden clarity that calmed him, he knew what he had to do. He needed to find Monica and kill her.

He smiled. Yes, that's what he had to do. And he started thinking of how to find her as if the information was there all the time just waiting for him to be calm enough to use it. Walking into the street again, he spotted his car. He knew now that he was on the perfect course. Why else would he find what he needed when he needed it?

Before getting in, he gathered all the trash from the interior. Every fast food bag, box, and napkin, every empty water bottle, cup, and cap. The coffee that had ended up in his car somehow was tossed away too, as were the extra things of aspirin and other headache remedies that had never worked. When he emptied the car of all trash, he folded the three blankets he'd acquired somehow and put them neatly on the seat. Taking out the mats, he shook each of them, including the ones in the front. When he was satisfied with his results, he got in, started the car, and waited for the warmth from the heater to penetrate his frozen body. By the time he pulled into traffic, he had it all worked out.

His first stop was to find a hotel. He didn't get the most expensive this time, but he did want one that had a lobby. Using the driver's license in his pocket that sort of looked like him, he handed it to the clerk. He didn't have any idea where it had come from, but now he didn't worry. He had a plan.

He loved lobbies in hotels with their shops and people coming and going. He got a room on the seventeenth floor and told the clerk that his luggage was coming later; he had a servant coming to bring it to him. After being shown his room, he left again. He had things to do.

He stopped at Wal-Mart and purchased some cheap jeans and some other things he needed. Underwear, socks, and t-shirts. He also picked up shampoo, soap, and a single piece of luggage. When he paid cash for these things, he realized that whatever he did, he had to do it quickly. He was down to his last hundred and forty dollars. Moving to the car again, he loaded everything in his luggage and went to the hardware store.

Here he purchased rope, pliers, tape, and nails. He wasn't sure what he needed them for, but when he'd walked by them, he had felt the need to pick them up. By the time he'd loaded these things into his case, he was down to less than a hundred dollars. Time to play.

It took him ten minutes of watching the CIA building to see the woman he was after. He didn't follow her directly home and had lost her twice. The only reason he had been able to figure out where she lived at all was because he'd taken a left when there had been a road barricaded off and had seen her car pull into a gated area. When he drove by the place slowly, he saw the big gate and realized it wasn't a gated community like where his parents lived, but a single residence. He pulled over his car down the street and walked to the gate. He slipped into the yard across the street from the big house and knocked on the door.

He looked around the neighborhood and saw that it was sparse when it came to houses. When the elderly woman opened the door, he pulled his gun up and shot her in the forehead. As she tumbled back, he stepped over her and dragged her lifeless body into the house with him. Closing the door, he left the woman lying where she was and went to the living room to spy on the gate just in front of him.

"Now we wait." He got up a few minutes later and got the meal that had been cooking in the microwave. He thanked the dead woman and ate it sitting in front of the window. Drinking the unopened bottle of water he'd found on the counter, he settled in to wait for Monica to come out. Two hours later, a limo pulled out.

Finding the old lady's keys, he went to the garage and got into her vehicle. He was pulling out when a second car came out of the gate. He could see that this one held who he was looking for and she was alone. Alone, he supposed, if you didn't count the dark sedan behind her. He didn't care. He had a plan.

~~~

Monica pulled into the dry cleaners ten minutes before they closed. The lady had told her that she had found something in her pocket and wanted to know if Monica could come and get it. She thought it had value, and as they had no safe, she wanted to make sure it was returned. It was the necklace that Khan had given her.

"One day," Monica mumbled to herself. "I have it one day and I lose it. Or nearly so. Damn it."

She didn't tell anyone where she was going except the guard on her tail. She had to tell him because, while she was embarrassed, she wasn't stupid. Besides, she was a little afraid after last night. She shivered while she drove and turned up the heat. She wondered if she'd ever be warm again.

The woman that had been killed last night had been another look alike. But this time, he'd taken his time with killing her. After who they all knew was Tony had tied her to a chair, he'd cut off all her hair. And not, the police had said, with a pair of scissors. He'd peeled her hair from her scalp as if he was scalping her.

He'd also raped her repeatedly with several different objects, the last being a knife. Caitlynne hadn't told them this part, but Monica had seen it in her mind. Had the woman not had her throat slit, she would have hemorrhaged to death from the wounds to her vagina. Tony's rage had escalated. And it was directed at her.

The lady at the dry cleaners was very nice. She'd asked about the necklace, and Monica had told her it was a wedding gift from her new husband. When the lady had remembered seeing her in the paper, she asked to have it signed. Monica waited at the counter for her to get it when she glanced out the window.

The sedan that had been following her was still there, but a man was walking away from it. She could see the window down on the car and thought that he'd been talking to them. The guards were very nice, and she didn't doubt they had plenty of friends around. She knew that these two men were from this area. By the time she had signed the newspaper article and collected her now clean dress, she went out the door and smiled at the car. She was in her own car when she felt something touch the back of her head. She heard Tony's laughter seconds before he spoke.

"You have been a very naughty girl, Monica. I have been looking for you for days and days. We had plans, you and I, and now you've messed them up." She glanced at the other car to try and get their attention. "Oh they won't be able to help you. I had to make sure that when I took you, I'd have you all for myself. They both died for you…because of you."

"Please don't do this. I just got married and I want to spend the rest of my life with…"

The pain exploded in her head. When he hit her, she slammed her head forward on the steering wheel. Blood poured from the wound as stars danced in front of her eyes.

"I want you to do just what I say and I won't have to kill anyone else because of you. You're going to drive correctly and do just what I tell you. If you don't, I'll shoot everyone we come across until you listen to me." She nodded and felt the gun press harder into her head. "Turn out of this parking lot and toward Stadium Street. Make a left there."

She drove for twenty-five minutes, knowing that if she did anything wrong or even looked at someone wrong, he would kill them. Terrified more than she'd ever been, she knew something was different about Tony. He was…she supposed the word would be confident, and seemed to have something completely worked out in his mind. She had a feeling that it was her being dead, and she wondered how she was going to get out of this.

Reaching out with her mind, she captured the mind of someone. She told him about the men at the dry cleaners. Since she was driving, she couldn't hold onto any one person for very long so she told six people the same thing.

"Dead men at Washington State Dry Cleaners. Have Monica." Over and over she would tell them and hoped that at least one of them would relay the information. When he had her pull up behind what she knew was his car, she turned off the engine to her car and knew that this was it. When he had her get into the passenger seat of his car, she dropped the necklace on the seat beside her and got out. There was no way she was letting him touch it.

She told six more people where to find her car. "Milner Street. Stolen car. Call police." Monica didn't know if that would really get her car stolen or someone would report it. She hoped someone would find it.

Monica expected him to shoot her as soon as they got in the car together. But he held the gun on her as he drove. When he started to sing to the music, she looked around for an opportunity to jump from the car. Then he reached over and grabbed her hand with his armed hand.

"You try anything and I will find a grade school, run this car into it, then shoot every child I see. You know that I'll do it too. I'm a man with a plan."

She nodded, terrified he'd do just that. She didn't want any more deaths because of her. He told her good girl and continued driving.

By the time they were pulling into the parking garage, she was nearly doubled over sick with terror. He held the gun to her as he took his suitcase out of the back seat and motioned for her to precede him. When they entered the hotel, she couldn't make her mind touch anyone else's. She was going to die was all that kept going through her mind. She was going to die one day after saying, "I do."

When he opened the door with his card, she walked into the room. She saw the suitcase go tumbling before pain exploded in her head again. This time, it took her to her knees. Before she could move away, a second blast of pain took her. As she was tumbling to the floor, she reached for anyone and touched the mind of Tony. Christ, he was going to make her suffer.

Chapter Seventeen

Khan was sitting at the table talking to his mom and dad when Caitlynne and his brothers came in. He knew immediately that something had happened. When he stood up, his mother leaned into him. He held her. Caitlynne told him to sit.

"I'd rather stand. I don't know what you have to tell me, but if I'm standing, I can fall to the chair. If I'm already there, I'll hit the floor." He was babbling. He knew it, and so did everyone else. "Please tell me she's still alive."

"As far as we know. There's no reason to believe he's killed her." He finally sat. "Someone called the...six people called the police about dead men at the Washington State Dry Cleaners. They were the men assigned to follow Monica. Both men were shot at close range by the same gun that killed two other people over the past two weeks. The callers had no idea why they called because, as they told the dispatcher, they didn't have any dry cleaning, but they had to call. Also, they were to tell us that someone had Monica."

"She contacted them."

Caitlynne nodded.

"So she is alive to do that. Was there...what else?"

"A stolen car was reported. On Milner Street. When the police arrived, they hadn't put the two incidents together yet and ran the plates on every car there. Luckily, there were only nine. None had been reported stolen, but Walker's car came up and that he was related to me. They called my office first and informed me what was going on. They also told me they found something in the front seat."

She handed him the necklace. Khan gripped it in his hand and looked up at Dylan when he touched his shoulder. He handed it to him when he'd asked. His brother held it tightly.

"She's afraid, terrified. She left this so that he wouldn't touch it. She is hoping that when this is over, you will put it back on her and love her." Dylan handed him the necklace. "If the emotion is really strong, I can get it. She is very frightened, but she's really pissed too. She isn't going to go down easy."

Khan didn't even ask. He knew that his brother had secrets that he would share when he wanted to. He thanked him and looked at Caitlynne. She looked grim.

"She'll get us to her. No matter how she has to do it. We'll find her. She managed to get us this far, she'll get us to her."

He believed it too. Khan didn't leave the kitchen. There was a phone there, and this room led out of the house and was closest to the garage. When she contacted someone else, he was going to be ready to go. He'd already taken Caitlynne's truck keys. He was going to be prepared when he went to get her.

Agents came in and out all afternoon. He watched them quietly and tried not to glare at them. He'd been told by his mother that he was scaring them. He had the look of a man posed on the edge. He felt that way too. The last time he'd stood up when one of them were in the room, the man actually put his hand on his gun. It might have been funny if he wasn't so afraid.

It was four hours later when he received a phone call. The cook had answered the phone and handed it to him without saying anything. He asked if it was Monica, and the man shook his head. He said hello, and the man at the other end sounded confused.

"I'm at the Wilkinson Hotel. I'm not real sure why you want to know that, but I just called to let you know." Khan asked him who he was. "Tim Daily. Do I know you?"

Khan hung up on him. Some idiot trying to get something from his family, no doubt, or had read about the wedding in the paper. He was just sitting back down when the phone rang again. The cook handed it to him again.

"Hey, I don't think I know you, but I'm staying at the Wilkinson Hotel. Out off Walden Road. You know where that's at?"

Khan hung up. He heard the phone ring before he stepped away and reached for it before the cook could. He didn't have time for this shit. Dylan walked in just as he blasted the man.

"Look, buddy, I don't give a shit where you are or where you work. We need this line open for important calls." He slammed the phone down and looked at the cook. "If anyone else calls that line, tell them we're using it for the police. Maybe that'll stop them."

"Did Monica ever use this phone?"

Khan looked at his brother and shrugged. He asked the cook the same question.

"Yes. She wanted to make a few phone calls this morning to go and get her dry cleaning." The cook frowned. "That number is private. No one else has it but the staff, and I guess Miss Monica."

The phone rang again. This time Khan reached for it with a shaky hand. When he said hello this time, he had a pen and paper shoved at him from Dylan. The person at the other end wanted to speak to Bill, the cook. He took it.

It was about an order he'd placed. He hurried through the conversation and hung up. He stepped back when Khan asked him too. The phone rang twice more, but it was for the staff. He looked at the agent when he walked in.

"I think she's at the Wilkinson. There have been several calls of people telling us that they're there. I don't know if she's actually there, but she might be."

The man nodded and walked out. Caitlynne walked back in a minute later.

"I think she's there. Can we go and get her?"

"Not yet. My men are checking to see if someone fitting the description has checked in with a woman. We can't go in and close the place down without all our Ts crossed." An hour later, they said that no one had checked in under the name of Barr and that no one had come in with a woman in the past three days.

Khan slumped in the chair. "It has to be her. Why would those people call and tell us where they were if not for her asking them to?" Caitlynne said she didn't know. "I have to have her back, Caitlynne. She's all I have in the world."

"We'll get her. When someone calls again, I want you to pump them for everything they know. Maybe she told them something else or they got the name wrong. I don't think so, but she's not there."

He nodded. He knew she was, and short of going door to door of the hotel, there was nothing really he could do. He watched the phone, and every time it rang, everyone in the room tensed up. He was ready to go out and find her himself until Dylan came in the room again and sat down. Each of them came to sit with him each hour, and he wondered if when the time came, they'd be going with him to get her or try to stop him. He hoped it was the former because he didn't want to have to kill them if it was the latter.

~~~

Screaming in her head woke her. She didn't know who it was at first, but soon realized it was her. He was hurting her again. He was taking great pleasure in this, and she was sure that he was going to kill her sooner rather than later. She was so weak, but reached for someone to help her.

"Tell Khan to come where you are now to get me. I'm on the seventeenth floor. Hurry. I'm dying." She gave them the phone number to the kitchen at the house. She wished she'd paid more attention to what the name of the hotel was now, but she'd been so afraid.

The knife slid into her again. She screamed around the gag, this time biting it hard enough that she felt blood, her blood, fill her mouth. She looked up at Tony with her one eye, the other long since swollen shut.

"If you'd just tell me that you love me, I will end this. You know you do and that you've made a mistake marrying that other man. You just have to tell me." He cut her again, and she felt faint with it. She reached for someone else, anyone else, and screamed at him rather than asking for help.

Please, she begged him in her mind. *Please just get it over with.*

~~~

The phone rang and Khan stepped to it. His heart was in his throat and he was shaking. He felt his hand being taken and looked over at his dad. He nodded, and Khan picked up the receiver.

"I'm looking for Khan. Is he there?" He told the man that he was him. "She said to tell you to hurry. She's on the seventeenth floor. She said that she's dying for you to hurry."

"Where are you?" the man cried out. "Sir? Are you there? What's happening? Tell me."

"She screamed at me. Just now she screamed and it sounded like she's in a great deal of pain. I'm calling the desk and seeing—"

"Don't do that. He might kill her if they call up there. He's dangerous. I'm coming. Are you at the Wilkinson?" The man told Khan he was. "I'm coming. We're all coming, but stay away from the floor. He'll kill you both. He's killed so many others."

The man assured him that he would and told him that he'd be near the elevators when he arrived. "I just checked in on the fourteenth. I can…I have the ability to talk to others and I heard her loud and clear. I'll be waiting."

Khan hung up and turned to his dad again. In the time he'd answered the phone, his entire family was standing there with their coats on. The cook, a big, burly man, had his on as well.

"You'll not go without me. I know what you people are, and while I can appreciate the situation, I like this girl, and I'm going with you." He looked over at Walker. "You try and stop me and I'll quit this house and go anyway. I'm going."

No one said a word as they went out to the cars. Khan was riding with his brother in Caitlynne's truck. Just where he wanted to be. The others were in two other vehicles including Bill's. The man had his own little arsenal in his trunk, it seemed.

The ride was one of the slowest and longest of his life. When they pulled in front, there were several SUVs already there, and they were leading people out. There was a scare of a large animal loose in the building. He looked at Caitlynne.

"I didn't know what you'd do so I wanted a cover story first. It's been in the works to be told to the public since she was kidnapped." She kissed his cheek before moving into the building. "Try not to fucking eat one of my agents. I like most of them, and the ones I don't, I'll give you a list later."

He nodded as they moved to the elevator. Walker and Dylan were with them. The man who had called, Daniel Patterson, was there as well, and he was armed. The man looked like he could eat them for breakfast. And he was a werebear.

"You go on up and find her. You leave this down here to me. I will keep anyone from coming down without your say so." He looked at Dylan, and there seemed to be some sort of understanding between them. "I'll let him know if the elevators move before you let me know."

As soon as the doors shut, Caitlynne pulled out her gun, stood under the small camera, and shot it. She winked at him. He took off his shirt and told her to turn around. When she laughed at him, he turned to Walker who only shrugged. She was going to get her butt beat. He knew it.

By the time she, the other two, and he were on the floor, he and Walker both had shifted. Caitlynne was going ahead of them to get all the people out on the floor. Dylan walked by each door and paused. He said he would be able to find her.

They walked slowly down the hall. There were eleven rooms on each side of the hall, and Dylan stopped at each one. When he would pause too long, he would shake his head and whisper that it was occupied. He and Walker would hide around the corner until Caitlynne got them roused and off the floor. They remembered to contact Bill each time.

The fourth time he paused too long, Khan started down the hall. Stupid fucking people should learn to listen. When a soft whistle had him turning, Dylan took off his shirt. She was in there.

Caitlynne stood in front of the door. "I'm going to unlock the door and when I do, I'm going to step back. If possible, I would like very much not to have to explain what went down in here. The bedrooms are on the left and the right. He probably has her in one of them."

Khan snarled for her to get a move on and she swiped the card to unlock the door. He waited for her to move back. No one wanted her hurt either. She set the large, black bag down that he hadn't even noticed that she had and nodded. He looked at Walker, who had shifted back to human.

"She's going to need me to help her. You have a problem with that?"

Khan shook his big head.

"Good. And Khan? She's going to be hurt. I need for you to make sure you know that I'm only going to be helping her."

Khan told him he understood. He looked at the now open door. He had to go in, and he wasn't looking forward to seeing what that monster had done to her. He nosed the door open and entered the room on silent paws. They all moved to the bedroom to the right. The door was shut. When Dylan walked up to it and shook his head, they turned to the other door. The door was shut here as well.

Dylan shifted. He nodded to the door, and Khan was poised, ready to leap inside the moment it opened. When he turned the knob, Dylan stepped back and moved out of the way. The scream that rent the air made him knock the door back and leap in the room.

Christ, he was going to kill her. Blood was on the walls, over the bed. The smell of impending death filled the air. There were footprints in the carpet, bloodied and large. Booted and barefooted. A dress and a bra were there also covered in blood.

Khan

Khan moved forward to see her. He needed to see her in the worst way. When he was perhaps only ten feet away, Khan froze for a second, no more, but the man turned. The blood on his shirt was fresh and the knife in his hand dripped with blood, her blood. Khan snarled deep, his claws burst from his paws, and he moved toward the man. When he was less than five feet away, he leapt at him. Khan hit him with all his weight.

He felt the sharp blade enter his shoulder, then his hip. He couldn't seem to get a good hold on the man. When the man raised his arm up to give Khan what would be a killing blow to the heart, he lunged for his throat. He clamped his powerful jaws into his neck just as he clawed at the man's soft belly.

The smell of feces and urine permeated the air. The man's screams rang in his ears, but Khan didn't let him go; he tore at the man. Jerking his head to and fro until he felt the flesh give and fresh blood flood his mouth, he knew he'd torn his throat out. Khan wanted more than his death; he wanted him gone for good. He snapped his mouth over his neck again and felt the bone break under his strength. The man's head rolled off and away from the body just as Khan dropped it.

He turned to the bed to see his brother over his mate. He snarled, the taste of fresh blood in his mouth, the adrenaline still coursing through his body hard and hot. Khan was ready to leap at him, to kill the man who dared touch his mate. But a sudden movement had him stop. He couldn't harm the female.

"You take one more step forward and I will blow your fucking brains out." Caitlynne held the gun steadily at his head. "I mean it, Khan. You back the fuck up and take a chill pill or so help me, I will kill your fucking ass."

"I'd do it, man. You don't want to fuck with her. She's breeding and could—"

Walker cut Dylan off. "Khan, shift. I need you to…shift, please."

Khan found he didn't want to. He wanted to leap at Walker and have Caitlynne kill him. He shook his head and looked at Walker again. He nodded and Khan knew that they were too late.

"I can't save her. She's dying. The loss of blood is tremendous. She won't make it to the elevator, much less to the hospital." Dylan handed him a pair of pants as Walker continued. "He stabbed her so many times, did so much damage, I don't know how she's hung on this long."

"You have to do something. You have to save her." Khan went to the side of the bed and looked down at her. She was a mess. Her body and bed were so bloodied, he couldn't tell where she was. He looked up at Walker when he cleared his throat.

"You could try to save her by converting her."

Khan shook his head.

"It's her only chance. If you—"

"She'll die. I can't do that to her, she'll—"

"She's going to die anyway. Try it, Khan. It's her only hope. If you don't do it, she will surely die. But if she makes it, you've saved her life."

Khan felt the tears on his face. He was asking him to kill her. He couldn't do it. He wouldn't. He took her hand in his and kissed it. He looked up at Walker and shifted again.

Chapter Eighteen

Walker felt for his brother. He knew as well as the rest of them did that converting a human to a cat was nearly a death warrant for them. When Khan shifted and bit down hard into Monica's belly, he cringed. She would either die immediately or she'd start the change. Walker reached for his own mate's hand and held it as he listened to Monica's heart slow even more.

"I've opened the room across the hall. It's empty of anything that might belong to a guest. I know that time is running out for us, so we have to figure out a way to get them over there." Dylan came into the room once more and looked at him. "Walker, can we move her?"

"No. Not just yet. We need just a little more time." He listened again and held his breath. Her heart was slower, nearly five seconds between each beat. He knew that when they moved her, they would be moving a dead woman. Then he heard it. A stutter of a beat, then another.

"What is it?"

He looked up at Caitlynne and smiled when her heart started beating faster. Not like it should, but it was getting stronger. He nodded.

"We can move her now, but Khan, you stay with us. We'll take the sheet, each of us taking a corner. Khan, don't

185

you dare stop giving her your essences. If you do, we might lose her yet." They each took a corner and froze when someone knocked on the door. It was Bill.

It took him only seconds to see what they were doing, and he dropped his gun and took Caitlynne's corner from her. They had her and Khan going through the doorway in seconds. It had been tricky for a second, but Bill had suggested Khan climb on the sheet with her and they got them across the hall. They had to put the sheet on the floor and drag it so they wouldn't lose them both, but it worked.

Laying her on the bed, each man stood by while Walker listened to her heart again. He felt tears roll down his cheeks, and he was unable to speak for the lump in his throat. He nodded and held his wife to him. "Her heart is slow, still very slow, but it's getting stronger. I don't fucking know how, but she's might just make it."

Caitlynne hugged him and took off. She had work to do as well.

Khan shifted again and they both sat next to her. Her chances were better of making it, but she still had to shift. If they could bring her around and get her to shift, then she'd heal much quicker. And her loss of blood would make her weak. Walker thought of his own mate's conversion and decided that the next time he saw her, he was going to fall at her feet and tell her over and over how much he loved her.

"The man, do you think anyone will believe that he was mauled by a wild animal and the animal got away?"

Walker looked at his brother.

"I wouldn't."

"Neither would I, but Caitlynne will make them believe it. And she said that having to shoo those other idiots out will help. She told them that the animal was spotted on this floor. I think her plan is to tell them that they found Barr like that and leave it at that."

Khan nodded. "Is she going to be pissy with me for long? I didn't exactly do what she told me to do. She said that I could kill him, but not make it too messy. The CIA was picking up the bill."

Walker laughed a little, needing it as much as his brother did. "I think she'll get over it soon enough. I'm going to tell her that it's a cat thing." He listened to her heart again. It was still slow and not any worse than before. He wrapped some of the wounds, and stitched two of them up until Khan asked him to stop. It was hard for him to let him touch her without hurting him.

"It won't matter anyway. When she shifts, they'll be gone." Walker looked at his brother. "Would you have killed me? In there when I was helping her, would you have killed me?"

Khan looked at him, and Walker could see the answer in his eyes. He would have. He would have killed him and they both knew it. When Khan looked back at Monica, he spoke softly.

"I hate myself for that. You warned me that you were going to help her and that I needed to back off. But that man had hurt her and I…the kill was still on my mind and in my heart. His blood was still coursing through me. I saw you standing over her and…" Khan looked from Walker to her and back to him. "I would ask that you forgive me, but I can't forgive myself. I would have killed you without thought to anything other than having you dead."

Walker didn't say anything. He and Khan would have to talk again about this, but not now. First of all, he wouldn't listen to him. No matter what he said or how much he told his brother that he had already forgiven him, he wouldn't listen.

Maybe never would. Secondly, he knew that in order for him to heal from this, it was going to take the love of the woman lying between them. If she lived, and Walker had to believe that she would, then Khan would be a better man than he'd ever been.

He heard the commotion down the hall. Neither of them moved when there were shouts and orders being given for the rooms to be evacuated. Caitlynne told him to stay put through their connection, that no one would enter that room but her. He heard the door open and close a few minutes later and Caitlynne walked in. He shook his head at her.

"They have cleared the floor and no sign of an animal. They've declared Barr dead at the scene and are currently looking for a female that may or may not have been murdered in the room by him." She looked at Khan. "You doing okay?"

"Yes. She's still with me."

Caitlynne nodded.

"I can't leave her just yet if you need me to go downtown."

She looked at Walker and then back at Khan. "You think I turned you in? Not fucking likely. She's going to kick your ass bad enough when she finds out you made another big decision without consulting her first. She is mighty picky about that."

Khan laughed and then nodded. "I can't wait to hear it. I plan on reminding her of this daily so I can hear her yell at me for it. I deserve it. I think that I will welcome it."

Caitlynne snorted. "I wouldn't tell her that, if I were you. She might just find other ways of kicking your ass to the curb if you did. Khan, she's going to be fine. She's entirely too stubborn and pigheaded to die. Especially at that bastard's hand. We both know that."

Walker checked her heart again. It had improved and he told them both. When he took her blood pressure, he noted that it was up as well. He breathed a sigh of relief and looked at his brother. "Mom and Dad want to come up. They have been in constant contact with me since Dylan went down to them. Mom said she wants to come up and bring you something to eat and some things for Monica. She said that she'll need some clothes when she wakes."

Khan brushed the hair from her forehead and nodded. "She'll want a shower too. I know that I want one as well. I need to get the stench of that man off me."

Caitlynne left, saying that she would see what she could do to get them up. Walker had a feeling they'd be coming up in a uniform if she had to sneak them past security and her men. An hour later, the door opened again and his mom and dad were there.

~~~

Khan left her to take a shower. Somehow, he had extra towels and other things to clean up with and decided that Caitlynne was going to get a better gift than the one he'd picked out for her for Christmas. The bracelet with hers and Walker's initials on the pendent didn't seem like enough to thank the woman who had saved his mate.

He had no doubt that Walker was a good doctor, but all the doctoring in the world wouldn't have gotten him in the room to kill the bastard that had hurt his mate. Nor did he doubt that she was pulling some major shit to get not only his family up there, but everything they needed to make their stay easier.

The water ran red when he stepped under the spray. He scrubbed his body with the wash rag, then tossed it out of the stall and into the sink when he washed himself the second time. He was on his forth wash cloth when he felt clean enough to wash his hair and his body again. He wondered if he'd ever feel clean again.

He pulled on the clean pants that his mother had bought for him. There was a shirt in the bag, as well as some underwear and socks. She'd forgotten shoes, she'd told him, and would bring them later. He didn't care now; he was clean and feeling better than he had for hours.

She was still unconscious now seven hours later. Walker had told him that she might need all that time to convert, and he was no longer checking her heartbeat every five minutes. When he declared her well, Khan let him close a few of the wounds on her body that were bleeding still and had to walk out of the room only twice so he wouldn't hurt him. When he came out of the bathroom, his mother was washing Monica's face and arms.

"She'll feel better once she wakes if she's not all covered in blood, don't you think?" He helped her by picking Monica up gently so the sheets could be changed. He held her for a few minutes longer before putting her on the fresh linens.

"I killed that man." His mother looked up at him when he spoke. "I did it and I'd do it all over again if I had the chance."

"Of course you would. You love her." She sat back in the chair after handing him a large sandwich, which he told her he didn't want. "Eat it. You'll need your strength for when she wakes."

He took a bite and it felt as if he stomach woke from a long nap. He ate the sandwich so quickly that she handed him another. He ate this one slower and drank three bottles of the water that had been in the small refrigerator. His dad showed up to trade places with his mom so she could go and get some things from the store.

"She'll buy it out, no doubt. She loves this woman. So do I." Khan nodded at his dad as he continued. "When I was younger, I killed a man once. He'd been hurting your mother."

Khan looked up at him. "Someone was messing with Mom? When was this? I don't remember that."

His dad nodded. "You were small and Dylan was about a year old. This man had been coming around looking for work and there hadn't been any around the town. Your mom didn't tell me that he sometimes came during the day when I was gone, but when he touched her, I knew."

His dad touched the sheet over Monica, but not her skin. His dad would understand more than any other about touching her right now. But he did go on with his story.

"He'd hit her with his fist in the arm. I don't remember why now or how he'd done it, but I'd felt her pain and her fear. She'd had you take the boys out to the barn to hide when she saw him coming. By the time I'd gotten there, he'd ripped open her blouse and had tried to rape her. She couldn't shift to hand him his ass because of the band he'd tied her up with. She was furious and kicking out at him whenever he got near enough for her to kick. When I came in, my cat took one look at the situation and took me."

Khan waited, knowing that this would be hard for his dad. His father hated for anyone to use their strength over another and this would have been no different for him. But his mate was hurt and the man responsible was still hurting her.

"I tore him off her. He'd managed to get past her when I came in the house. I was a mite younger then and didn't have any problem taking him down. He was so shocked he shit himself. Didn't stop me, though. I tore his throat out and spit it in his face." His dad looked at him. "Never thought to just scare him away. Never even occurred to me to simply wound him and have him run along. I wanted him dead, and that's what I did. To this day, I don't regret my actions. And as surely as I'm sitting here, I tell you I never will."

"I could have stopped when I killed him," Khan admitted to his father now. "I could have stopped at tearing his throat out and walked away. But I wanted more, needed more than that. He'd not just hurt her, but he'd nearly killed her."

His dad nodded and sat there for several minutes before he spoke again. "She'll forgive you if that's what you're worried about. She'll have no regrets at all that you killed him. She might be a tad pissy when she finds out she's a cat. Not at being the cat, mind you, but because you did one of those major decision things she said you need to discuss together. I know and you know that she was a mite under the weather when it came to asking, but she ain't going to be happy about you going ahead and doing it."

Khan told his dad that Caitlynne had told him the same thing. And he told his dad basically the same answer he'd given Caitlynne.

"Yeah, well, I can see her being a bit mad over you thinking you had a choice in the matter. She's a lot like your mom on that score. She's a fine woman. Gonna be a better cat too. I can't wait to see the kids she has. Fine bunch of boys she'll have too." His dad snorted when he suggested that he'd be a part of them. "No, she'll raise them to be like her. Full of life and sunshine. Fine boys. This family had boys to carry on the line, as it should be."

Khan didn't tell his dad that he wanted a daughter like her. Just exactly like her. He held her hand and gave her his warmth and love. Khan wanted her to wake. He wanted her to yell at him and to love him. Anything but this sleep she was in.

The bleeding had stopped, Walker told him, two hours later. He said that if Khan wanted to, they could move her to the house where she would be home when she woke. Khan asked if she still needed to shift before being moved and Walker shook his head.

"She's healing like she has already. Some of the smaller wounds are already gone, and there doesn't seem to be any scarring. I would say that she is going to make a full recovery no matter where she is, and taking her to the house is the best thing for all of us."

Khan agreed, and they found a way to get her out of the hotel without involving her in the murder that had taken place just down the hall from her. Caitlynne told the press that it was a woman who had fallen in the shower and nothing at all to do with the cat being on the loose. When they'd taken her down to the ambulance, Daniel was standing there speaking with the press. Caitlynne said that he was going to say that he'd found her when she hadn't shown up for their date. She was not identified until her husband could be notified of the accident.

When they were in the ambulance, Khan looked at Walker. He laughed. The man was just full of information on his wife's supposed affair.

"It was Daniel's idea. He said that he'd been on a case once when someone had called in that he couldn't get in touch with his girlfriend, his married girlfriend, he'd gone there to meet. The guy had said he was there to have an affair with a woman and she wouldn't answer his calls or his knocks at the door. It took the hotel staff a little too long to get to her, and the woman died from her injuries. Daniel said he'd play the part of the male so long as you knew that he'd never touch her."

"You assured him that I wouldn't, I suppose."

Walker nodded and laughed again.

"What does he want in return for his help? Money?"

"Nope. He just wants to come over to the property sometimes and have a good run. He said it had been so long since he'd seen another shifter as comfortable about their second skin as we were that he knew he could trust us not to make a rug out of him the first time he came around. I assured him that we were allergic to bear, and the meat was usually tough and stringy."

Khan laughed. It felt good, and he enjoyed a second laugh when he told him the trouble that Dylan was in right now. Apparently, their brother had made a pass at the wrong woman and was right now being yelled at by their mother.

"She was telling him that if he couldn't keep it in his pants, he might want to consider getting neutered. She said while she didn't think it would stop him, it might slow him down a little."

Khan doubted that anything would slow down Dylan and wondered aloud what would happen to the man when he found his mate and he could no longer cat around, pun intended.

"Don't know, but I can't wait to find out." Walker and he were still laughing about it when they pulled in front of the house. Instead of letting her be taken up on a gurney, Khan picked Monica up and carried her up to the bedroom himself. He needed to hold her, and stripped down after everyone left and crawled into bed with her. He held her to him and closed his eyes. Sleep claimed him almost immediately.

Chapter Nineteen

Monica woke slowly. She was afraid, actually, and didn't want to wake Tony if he was still in the room with her. She opened one eye and looked around the room, knowing instantly where she was. She heard the shower running and knew that Khan was in there. She sat up, wanting to see how much damage Tony had done to her.

She was still staring at her belly when Khan came out of the bathroom. She looked up at him and knew that whatever had happened had been a lot worse than she thought it had been. He looked pale and upset.

"Let me explain. There was no other—"

"Is he...did you kill him?" Khan nodded and dropped his head. "Look at me, please."

He did, and she could see the pain in his face. "I had no choice. Well, that's not entirely true. I did have one, but I didn't like it, so I killed him. I killed him because I could and because he'd hurt you."

She nodded. She would have done the same thing if he'd been hurt. But she could tell there was more and waited for him to speak. When he didn't, she did. "I was dying. I knew it too." He nodded. "He, Tony, said that he wanted me to tell him that I loved him and that I'd made a mistake by marrying you. And since I know that I didn't, I can only assume that you saved me, gave me some sort of miracle drug, and here I am. Mended and well. But that's not true, is it?"

He looked at her and she knew what he'd done. Her breath caught at what she saw in his mind. Khan walked toward her and sat on the edge of the bed.

"There was no way for you to make it to the hospital. Walker tried his best, but I knew that…Walker told me either I converted you and you died, or you died in that hotel room with Barr's body close by." He looked away. "I didn't want to, but if you died, I wanted it to be because we'd done everything we could to save you."

She thought about being a cat. That didn't bother her. None of it did really. Not even knowing that Khan had killed the man who had tried to kill her. She reached for his hand and he pulled away from her and stood up.

"I know that we should have talked about this. There really wasn't any time. You were dying. I couldn't live without you. Had you been lost to me, I would have attacked Walker when I could and had Caitlynne shoot me like she threatened to."

Monica was going to have to get more details on that later. Right now, her mate was hurting and she could fix it. "So you bit me and made me what you are. And no, we hadn't discussed it because you refused to even consider it. And then you go and do it without as much as a simple question to me." He started pacing the room and she knew that she had to do this to him. "What were you thinking? That I'd just say thank you, Khan, for saving my life and making me into something else?"

He didn't answer, but she could feel his anger. When she told him to stop pacing and answer her, she could see the anger vibrate off him. He was as pissed as she'd ever seen him.

"I did what I had to do." He stretched his neck, something she knew he did when he was nearing his breaking point. "You were dying and I did what I needed to do to save you. End of discussion."

She leapt out of the bed and went to stand in front of him. He tried to walk around her, but she shoved him, a little too hard, into the dresser behind him. When he growled at her, she growled right back.

"I'll say when it's finished. This is my body and my life you changed, was it not?" He nodded. "Then we have things to talk about. Like what were you thinking?"

He put his hands on her shoulders. For all his apparent anger, he was gentle, his hands barely gripping her. Khan's eyes were darker in the passion of his anger at her, but she knew that when he blew, he would never hurt her.

"You were dying. I had to—"

"Bullshit. Tell me why you did it." She waited, wondering if she should push him more. Before she could ask again, he kissed her.

The kiss was passionate, not hurtful. She wrapped her arms around his neck and held him to her as he took and took. When he lifted his head, he looked calmer; he even smiled.

"I did it because I couldn't stand the thought of living another day without you. I did it because I need you. Now and forever. I did it because, even though you drive me insane most of the time, I love you more than I've loved anyone in my life." He kissed her again. "I do love you. I'm so sorry for what I did to you. I knew that we should have—"

"Khan? Shut up and make love to me. With me. Please?"

"Gladly." He picked her up and carried her to the bed. When he stood over her and started taking off his shirt, she sat up to watch him. She doubted that she'd ever get bored seeing him naked. But before he took off his pants, he reached into his pocket, and sat down beside her.

"I was told you wanted me to put this back on you." She turned to look at him before he could put it around her throat. "Apparently, Dylan has a lot of things he can do that he's never shared with us."

She nodded. "I'm sure he does. He's a very quiet and reserved man, isn't he?"

"Yes. He's always been. I guess we know why now. He's been afraid that we'd feel differently about him if we ever found out just how much he knows." Khan turned her around and sat her over his lap. "But I don't want to talk about my brothers right now. I want to make love to my wife."

He took her mouth and rolled them so that she was on her back and he over her. When he took the neck of her shirt and ripped it from her, she watched his eyes, not what he was doing. She felt something move along her skin and looked up at him.

"It's your cat. She wants mine." He took her nipple in his mouth and nipped gently at it before lifting his head again. "When we get home, we're going to run in the woods behind my house and I'm going to let him have you. He wants to mark you both."

The next time her cat moved, she let her. Khan lifted his head from her breast again and looked down at her. His cat was close too. She could feel him.

"We're going to mess up this room if you keep that up. My cat wants to come out and play." Khan buried his face in her shoulder and she felt him purr. It moved along her body as if he was touching her.

"Khan, I can't...how do I keep her from coming out?" He laughed and stood up. "Khan?"

"Get a shirt on. We're going outside to play." He reached for his shirt and, on bare feet, padded to the door. "Hurry, Monica. The sun will be up soon and I would prefer that the household didn't see where we were going."

He walked out the door, and she sat there for a full second before she leapt from the bed to go after him. Grabbing up the first thing she touched, she went out the door after him.

~~~

Khan stood on the deck and waited for her. He was excited and knew that she was as well. When she wrapped her arms around him from behind, he put his hands over hers and held her.

"We'll need to be naked to keep us from having to enter the house without our clothes. We can shift with clothes on, but it tears them from us. We'll go out beyond those trees to do it." He felt her nod. "To shift, all you need to do is think about her coming to you. It won't hurt you. Maybe a slight discomfort the first time because she won't know what to do either. But when you want to shift back, just think of your human self and she'll flow over you like the cat will."

He could feel her nervousness and waited. He knew she had questions and would have many more after this. Khan was nervous too. He loved her and didn't want her to be afraid.

"Will she hurt you?" He started to laugh, but was glad he didn't when she continued. "She is making me think that she wants your blood. I don't know what that means really other than she wants to hurt you for whatever reason."

"She does. Not mine really, but my cat's. She wants to bond with him as much as mine does yours. They need to mark each other, and bloodletting and the scarring after is a way to show the world of other cats that we belong to each other." He turned to look down at her. "Are you ready?"

She nodded, and they walked hand in hand toward the trees. When she started to undress, she asked him another question. This one made him pause.

"When will I be in heat? Caitlynne said that's what it's called. She told me that you would know and that it happens four times a year." She glanced at him as she pulled off her pants. "I want a baby with you."

"Once you are in heat the first time, we'll both know when you're going into your time afterwards. When we have a child, you'll cycle around again, and we'll have to time it." When he was naked, he stood before her, his cock hard and aching. "When do you want to have a baby, Monica? Do you want to wait awhile?"

Naked, she came to him and wrapped her arms around him. When he cupped her ass and brought her flush against him, she lifted her legs and wrapped them around his waist. He rolled her over his cock several times, her juices coating him. He pressed her against the nearest tree and took her mouth. If they kept this up, they were never going to make it to the forest.

"I want a baby as soon as we can," she said against his throat. "The next time we are in heat, I want you to give me your child."

Khan lifted her up and brought her down hard onto his cock. She purred and he nearly came from the feeling it gave him. Moving in and out of her quickly, he brought her to a quick peak before setting her down and away from her. When she reached for him, he stopped her.

"No. I want to come inside of you as a cat. I want to take you to the ground and fuck you from behind. Shift for me, Monica. I want to see that beautiful cat of yours."

He watched her struggle with it. Khan knew that he could call her cat, but he also knew that it was painful that way, and he wanted her first experience to be as wonderful as he could make it, as they could make it. As she started to shift, her arms stretching and her fur beginning to appear, he watched as she went from a beautiful woman to an even more beautiful cat.

He dropped to his knees as she moved toward him. "Christ, baby, you're gorgeous. I've never seen a lovelier cat."

He rubbed her behind her ears and was rewarded with a deep purr. When she pawed at him, he let her take him to the ground and played with her. When she backed off, he stood up and watched her as he, too, shifted.

Their connection was immediate. He'd never been able to connect with her verbally as a human and hoped that her being a cat would help them. When she took off running ahead of him, he let her. They were safe here, and he promised himself that when they were home, he'd teach her that she had to keep up with him. There were predators even on their own land. When he felt her fear, he realized she'd gotten too far ahead and leapt after her.

"Stay back. He might hurt you." She had a large grizzly cornered and he wasn't thrilled about it. *"I said to stay—"*

When she sat down and cocked her head at the bear, he dropped down to his four paws as well. They seemed to be having a conversation, and Khan sat down as well. Daniel had asked to use this land too when he was in town and apparently had been given permission.

"He said that he knows me. He said that I contacted him when I was hurt." She looked back at him. *"He's a human."*

"Technically, he's a werebear. And yes. He called the house and told me that you'd contacted him when you were

hurt. He helped us find you when we did." Khan shivered when he thought of finding her as he had. *"He's one of the good guys."*

"So he says. He said that he can whoop my ass if I try to tackle him. Is that true?"

Khan stood up and looked at the giant of a bear. He had to weigh in at least seven hundred pounds. Her cat was probably a quarter of that if that much, and only because she was a were and not a regular panther.

"I think you can take him." She must have told Daniel what he said, because he growled at him. *"But not today. We have plans."*

He took off in the opposite direction of Daniel, and he knew that she followed him. He took her to a place he'd discovered a few days ago before all this had happened. As soon as he saw it again, he knew that she'd love it as well.

The lake was manmade, but no less beautiful. He sat on the edge of it and watched her walk around the bank next to him. She sat too and leaned her head against his. He could smell her now that they had stopped running, and he nipped at her muzzle. When she stood up, he came up behind her and put his paws to her shoulder. She dropped down, but not without snarling at him. His blood heated at her response.

No words were needed between them. It was as if they had been together forever. And Khan wanted forever with her. He pressed her down with his weight and felt her respond to him. As soon as she moved for him, he entered her deep and sank his teeth into her to hold her down.

Christ, he was so close already. He quickened his pace, knowing that as soon as he came in her, he was going to shift and take her again, this time as himself. As soon as she reared up and pressed back against him, he came. His cat snarled against her throat, and she back at him. Still, he wanted more of her.

"*Shift*," he commanded her, and watched as her body went from cat to human in one fluid motion. He nearly forgot to shift himself and was glad he waited when she lay before him naked. He buried his muzzle in her pussy and tasted her.

"Yes," she screamed at him as he lay down and drank more from her. He could taste her cream mixed with his cum and he wanted more. He flicked his tongue in her sheath and moaned. He wanted her to come this way, come in his mouth and let his cat taste all of her.

His cock was hurting, but he knew she was going to give him what he wanted. Her body was soaking him and the more he drank, he found he wanted more. When she screamed out her release, Khan lapped at her until he couldn't take it anymore. As soon as he pulled from her, he shifted and fell on top of her.

His cock entered her hard and when she wrapped her legs around him, he reached beneath her and tilted her more. He was as deep as he'd ever been. When she buried her nose in his shoulder, he felt his balls tighten. When she bit him, and he knew she would, he was going to come hard.

Her tongue teased him; her body heated him. Khan cupped her ass even as her teeth scraped along his throat. She was killing him, and he was more than willing to go this way. When her teeth sank deep in him, he slid his finger into her ass and felt his cock explode.

When her body tightened around him, his finger in her ass moved almost of its own accord. He felt her scream around his throat, her release as powerful as his own. Khan emptied himself in her over and over until he could feel his body drained. When he dropped over her, she came again, a small tremor that left him limp. Closing his eyes for a moment, he heard her giggle.

"You're wonderfully warm, but my ass is getting cold." He looked around and grinned at her. "Can you please roll to your back for a little while so I can thaw out?"

He stood up, pulling from her body reluctantly. Helping her to stand, he held her in his arms, rubbing his hands up and down her back to warm her. She looked up at him and he kissed her nose.

"I didn't think about the cold when I was deep inside of you. We should have brought a blanket." She snorted. "Okay, we should have brought two, but I've never wanted you like that before."

"Nor I you." She pulled away and started walking back to where they'd left their clothes. "Do you suppose we should have undressed here and then ended up here again? Might have saved us from walking through the forest—hey."

He shifted and ran past her. She came up behind him as her cat a few seconds later. They played a sort of tag all the way back to the spot where they'd started. As they dressed, he couldn't seem to stop touching her. They went into the house just when breakfast was being served.

Chapter Twenty

"Push, Caitlynne. Push and we'll have our baby."

Caitlynne glared at the doctor, then looked up at Walker. He was going to pay for this, he knew. He kissed her nose.

"I'm so not ever having another baby. You want them, you have it." She pushed through another contraction, and he handed her a teaspoon full of ice for her efforts. "And when this is over, if it ever is, I want dinner. A steak with all the trimmings."

He nodded. "Anything else? Maybe a pie for dessert? Or would you like a cake or two?"

She glared and pushed again when Doctor Edgar Hailing told her to. Walker was baiting her. He had to. She pushed better when she was pissed, and he was worried about how long this had been taking. So was Edgar.

"One more, darling, and you'll have your son. Big one too, I'd say." Caitlynne looked at him, and he put his hand over her mouth before she could blast the poor man again.

"Behave or you won't get anything but a peanut butter and jelly sandwich." She growled low, startling the doctor. "Behave."

Once more she pushed, and delivered their son. All ten pounds and four ounces of him. When Edgar laid him at her breast, the baby began rooting around looking for his lunch.

As soon as he found her nipple, he latched onto it as if he'd been doing it for years instead of this being his first time.

Caitlynne looked up at him, and Walker fell in love with his wife all over again. He kissed her mouth as the baby continued to eat. Touching his little head, he looked at his father and their bond was established. Father and son would be able to communicate even at his age. He sent his son his love.

"You going out to tell them about our kid?"

He was holding him now and didn't want to give him up just yet. He shook his head.

"Walker, give me our son and go and tell your family that he's okay. They're going to stampede this place if you don't."

She was right, and he handed him back to her. He kissed them both again and left the room. He was nearly to the waiting room when he saw his brother and his wife. Khan and Monica were going to have a baby too in a few more months.

He hugged his brother and kissed Monica. She was radiant. He walked with them to the room filled to overflowing with people there for his first child. He grinned at them all. "They're both fine. All his fingers and toes and weighed a little over ten pounds. Started nursing as soon as he found her breast. I think he's going to be hard to keep full." They all congratulated him, and he looked at his dad. "Wanna know his name now?"

"You know I do. I've been waiting on pins and needles for nearly five months on you. Shame on you for making an old man wait on such a monumental occasion. What if I had of died without knowing? What would you have done then?"

"Buried it on a sheet of paper for you. And we both know you weren't going to die with all these new babies coming around. You'd be making bargains with the Devil himself if you had to. That is if you're not already." Walker looked over at his mom. "Is he?"

"Hush up and tell us what his name is. I want to call him something besides Baby Bowen. You said when he was born you'd tell me." His father looked around the room. "Ain't that what he said?"

"What was said, you old fool, is that they would tell us all." His mom smiled at him as she continued. "How is our lovely Caitlynne? She didn't kill the doctor, did she? She can be a mite high-strung when she's upset."

Walker kissed his mom. "She's wonderful. And you're right, we both tell you. I came out to tell you we had a son and that we're all fine. As soon as she gets in her room, I'll be out to get you. He should be in the nursery by now."

Kissing her again on the cheek, Walker went back to his wife. She was alone and lying in the bed with her eyes closed. He quietly sat in the chair next to the bed. She looked over at him.

"Did he try to get the name?" He nodded with a laugh. "Old buzzard. Come here and kiss me. And where is my dinner?"

He'd had Khan order it as soon as they knew this was it. "It will be here at six. It's a quarter till now, so soon."

Walker climbed into the bed with her and held her. She was warm and soft, and he loved her very much. She soon dozed, and when the nurse came in, she smiled at him and told him that she had to check her. As soon as he moved, Caitlynne woke.

"I want to go home soon. Do you think you can arrange that? I want to be with you and our son at home. Please, Walker?"

He nodded and went to find the doctor.

Edgar was a were himself and knew that Caitlynne would get as good of care at home as she would here, and he allowed it. Within five hours, they were loading her up, and his dad was fussing at him the whole time.

He was really going to enjoy telling him when they got home. Walker was going to let the man hold his grandson and then tell him. He couldn't wait to let him know that he and Caitlynne were naming the baby, George, after him.

~~~

Khan drove to Walker's home with Monica beside him. Her belly was beginning to show now and he reached over and rubbed his hand over the small mound. She put her hand over his and held it there.

"You know what it is, don't you?" She nodded at him. "Don't tell me. I don't want to know. He's probably a boy. There haven't been anything but boys for nearly many generations."

She didn't say anything, but laid her head back against the seat. She looked so peaceful that when he stopped the car, he didn't want to wake her. She had been so tired lately.

"I love you." She woke and smiled at him. "I do more every day."

"And I love you too. This is going to be exciting for Walker and Caitlynne. I'm not surprised she didn't tell anyone, but Walker must have been about to bust knowing he knew something your dad didn't."

"Dad is pissed. He felt that instead of moving her, they should have told him the baby's name and then packed them up. He's going to have a brick if they wait much longer." Khan went around to the other side of the car to help her out. Even this early in the pregnancy, she was a little off balance. Just the first day of May and they had six and a half months to go. He could hardly wait.

When she fell asleep as soon as she sat down, he covered her up with a blanket. He smiled at Dylan when he said he'd sit with her. Khan went to get her some juice for when she woke up. When he returned, the two of them were laughing.

"Dylan said that I should tell you. He said you were worried."

Khan sat down hard.

"It's okay Khan. I swear it."

"Is it a girl or a boy?"

She nodded.

"I mean the baby we're having. Is it a girl or a boy?"

Dylan laughed and stood. "Think about it, big brother. I'm sure you'll get it soon."

Khan looked at Monica when he left them. She looked so happy that he wanted to—

"Shit. It's one of each."

She laughed and nodded again. Holy hell, they were having twins. Khan was suddenly very tired himself.

About the Author

Kathi Barton, author of the bestselling series Force of Nature, lives in Nashport, Ohio with her husband Paul. In addition to writing full time, Kathi likes to spend time with her eight grandkids, three children, and three children-in-laws. She writes to relax and have fun.

Her muse, a cross between Jimmy Stewart and Hugh Jackman, brings them to life for her readers in a way that has them coming back time and again for more. Her favorite genre is paranormal romance with a great deal of spice. You can visit Kathi on line and drop her an email if you'd like. She loves hearing from her fans. aaronskiss@gmail.com.

Follow Kathi on her blog:
http://kathisbartonauthor.blogspot.com/

www.ingramcontent.com/pod-product-compliance
Lightning Source LLC
Chambersburg PA
CBHW030316180626
46810CB00003B/1109